ALSO BY LIAN HEARN

EMPEROR OF
THE EIGHT ISLANDS

THE TALE OF SHIKANOKO · BOOK 1

EMPEROR OF THE EIGHT ISLANDS

LIAN HEARN

FARRAR, STRAUS AND GIROUX · NEW YORK

Farrar, Straus and Giroux
18 West 18th Street, New York 10011

Printed in the United States of America
Originally published in 2016 by Hachette Australia
Published in the United States by Farrar, Straus and Giroux
First American edition, 2016

Map by K1229 Design

Library of Congress Cataloging-in-Publication Data
Names: Hearn, Lian, author.
Title: Emperor of the Eight Islands / Lian Hearn.
Description: First American edition. | New York : Farrar, Straus and
    Giroux, 2016. | Series: The tale of Shikanoko series ; 1
Identifiers: LCCN 2015042559 | ISBN 9780374536312 (softcover) | ISBN
    9780374715014 (ebook)
Subjects: LCSH: Japan—History—1185–1600—Fiction. | BISAC:
    FICTION / Literary. | FICTION / Fantasy / Historical. | GSAFD:
    Fantasy fiction. | Adventure fiction. | Historical fiction.
Classification: LCC PR9619.3.H3725 E47 2016 | DDC 823/.914—dc23
LC record available at http://lccn.loc.gov/2015042559

Designed by Jonathan D. Lippincott

Our books may be purchased in bulk for promotional, educational,
or business use. Please contact your local bookseller or the Macmillan
Corporate and Premium Sales Department at 1-800-221-7945, extension
5442, or by e-mail at MacmillanSpecialMarkets@macmillan.com.

www.fsgbooks.com • www.fsgoriginals.com
www.twitter.com/fsgbooks • www.facebook.com/fsgbooks

10 9 8 7 6 5 4 3 2 1

Frail indeed must be
Cross threads of frost and drawn threads
Fashioned of dewdrops
For brocades in the mountains
Are woven only to scatter

—from *Kokin Wakashū: The First Imperial Anthology of Japanese Poetry*, translated by Helen Craig McCullough

THE TALE OF SHIKANOKO
LIST OF CHARACTERS

MAIN CHARACTERS

Kumayama no Kazumaru, later known as Shikanoko or
   Shika

Nishimi no Akihime, the Autumn Princess, **Aki**

Kuromori no **Kiyoyori**, the Kuromori lord

Lady **Tama**, his wife, the Matsutani lady

Masachika, Kiyoyori's younger brother

Hina, sometimes known as Yayoi, his daughter

Tsumaru, his son

Bara or Ibara, Hina's servant

Yoshimori, also Yoshimaru, the Hidden Emperor, **Yoshi**

Takeyoshi, also Takemaru, son of Shikanoko and
   Akihime, **Take**

Lady **Tora**

Shisoku, the mountain sorcerer

Sesshin, an old wise man

The **Prince Abbot**
Akuzenji, King of the Mountain, a bandit
Hisoku, Lady Tama's retainer

THE MIBOSHI CLAN
Lord **Aritomo**, head of the clan, also known as the
    Minatogura lord
Yukikuni no **Takaakira**
The **Yukikuni lady**, his wife
Takauji, their son
Arinori, lord of the Aomizu area, a sea captain
Yamada Keisaku, Masachika's adoptive father
Gensaku, one of Takaakira's retinue
Yasuie, one of Masachika's men
Yasunobu, his brother

THE KAKIZUKI CLAN
Lord **Keita**, head of the clan
Hosokawa no **Masafusa**, a kinsman of Kiyoyori
Tsuneto, one of Kiyoyori's warriors
Sadaike, one of Kiyoyori's warriors
Tachiyama no **Enryo**, one of Kiyoyori's warriors
Hatsu, his wife
Kongyo, Kiyoyori's senior retainer
Haru, his wife
Chikamaru, later Motochika, **Chika**, his son
Kaze, his daughter

Hironaga, a retainer at Kuromori

Tsunesada, a retainer at Kuromori

Taro, a servant in Kiyoyori's household in Miyako

THE IMPERIAL COURT

The **Emperor**

Prince Momozono, the Crown Prince

Lady Shinmei"in, his wife, Yoshimori's mother

Daigen, his younger brother, later Emperor

Lady Natsue, Daigen's mother, sister of the Prince Abbot

Yoriie, an attendant

Nishimi no **Hidetake**, Aki's father, foster father to
    Yoshimori

Kai, his adopted daughter

AT THE TEMPLE OF RYUSONJI

Gessho, a warrior monk

Eisei, a young monk, later one of the **Burnt Twins**

AT KUMAYAMA

Shigetomo, Shikanoko's father

Sademasa, his brother, Shikanoko's uncle, now lord of the
    estate

Nobuto, one of his warriors

Tsunemasa, one of his warriors

Naganori, one of his warriors

Nagatomo, Naganori's son, Shika's childhood friend, later one of the **Burnt Twins**

AT NISHIMI
Lady Sadako and **Lady Masako**, Hina's teachers
Saburo, a groom

THE RIVERBANK PEOPLE
Lady Fuji, the mistress of the pleasure boats
Asagao, a musician and entertainer
Yuri, **Sen**, **Sada**, and **Teru**, young girls at the convent
Sarumaru, **Saru**, an acrobat and monkey trainer
Kinmaru and **Monmaru**, acrobats and monkey trainers

THE SPIDER TRIBE
Kiku, later Master Kikuta, Lady Tora's oldest son
Mu, her second son
Kuro, her third son
Ima, her fourth son
Ku, her fifth son
Tsunetomo, a warrior, Kiku's retainer
Shida, Mu's wife, a fox woman
Kinpoge, their daughter

Unagi, a merchant in Kitakami

SUPERNATURAL BEINGS
Tadashii, a tengu
Hidari and **Migi**, guardian spirits of Matsutani
The dragon child
Ban, a flying horse
Gen, a fake wolf
Kon and **Zen**, werehawks

HORSES
Nyorin, Akuzenji's white stallion, later Shikanoko's
Risu, a bad-tempered brown mare
Tan, their foal

WEAPONS
Jato, Snake Sword
Jinan, Second Son
Ameyumi, Rain Bow
Kodama, Echo

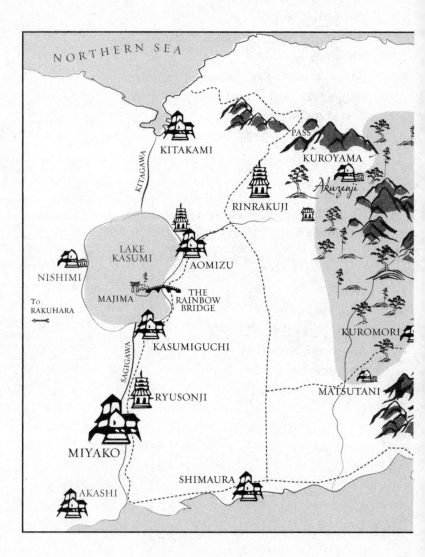

THE SNOW
COUNTRY

THE
DARKWOOD

Shisoku

MUENJI

KUMAYAMA

MINATOGURA

KUMAGAWA

ENCIRCLED SEA

----- ROADS

——— RIVERS
AND STREAMS

CONVENT
OR TEMPLE

HUT

SHRINE

ESTATE

TOWN

EMPEROR OF
THE EIGHT ISLANDS

KAZUMARU

"Did you see what happened?"

"Where is your father?" Two men were standing above him, their shapes dark against the evening sky. One was his uncle, Sademasa, the other Nobuto, whom he didn't like.

Kazumaru said, "We heard a funny noise," and he mimed placing stones on a board. "Clack, clack, clack. Father told me to wait here."

The men had come upon the seven-year-old hidden in ·the long grass, in the sort of form deer stamp out for their fawns. The horses had nearly stepped on him. When his uncle lifted him up the grass had printed deep lines on his cheek. He must have been there for hours.

"Who brings a child on a scouting mission?" Nobuto said quietly.

"He can't be separated from him."

"I've never seen a father so besotted!"

"Or a child so spoiled," Sademasa replied. "If he were mine . . ."

Kazumaru did not like their tone. He sensed their mockery. He said nothing but resolved to tell his father when he saw him.

"Any sign of his horse?" Sademasa asked Nobuto.

The older man looked toward the trees. "The tracks lead up there."

A small group of stunted trees clung to the side of the volcanic mountain. Some were dying, some already stumps. The air smelled of sulfur, and steam hissed from vents in the ground. The men went warily forward, their bows in their hands. Kazumaru followed them.

"Cursed-looking place," Nobuto said.

The larger tree stumps were crisscrossed with faint lines. A few black stones, a handful of white shells were scattered on the ground.

"Something bled here." Nobuto pointed at a splash on a pale rock. He crouched and touched it with his finger. "Still wet."

The blood was dark, almost purple.

"Is it his?" Sademasa whispered.

"Doesn't look human to me," Nobuto replied. He sniffed his finger. "Doesn't smell human either." He wiped his hand on the rock and stood, looked around, then suddenly shouted, "Lord Shigetomo! Where are you?"

You, you, you, came back the echo from the mountain, and behind the echo another sound, like a flock of birds beating their wings.

Kazumaru looked up as the flock passed overhead. He saw it was made up of strange-looking beings, with wings and beaks and talons like birds, but wearing clothes of a sort, red jackets, blue leggings. They looked down on him and pointed and laughed. One of them brandished a sword in one hand, a bow in the other.

"Those are his weapons," Nobuto cried. "That is Ameyumi."

"Then Shigetomo is dead," Sademasa said. "He would never have surrendered the bow alive."

Afterward, Kazumaru was not sure what he remembered and what he had dreamed. His father and his clever, witty mother often played Go in the long, snowbound winters at Kumayama. He had grown up with their sounds, the quiet clack of stones on the boards, the rattle in the wooden bowls. That day he and his father heard them together. They had ridden far ahead of the others. His father always liked to be in the lead, and the black horse was strong and eager. It had been a present from Lord Kiyo-yori, to whom the family were vassals and on whose orders they had ridden so far north.

His father reined in the horse, dismounted, and lifted him down. The horse began to graze. They walked through the long grass and almost stepped on the fawn, lying in its form. He saw its dark eyes, its delicate mouth, and then it was on its feet and leaping away. He knew the other men would have killed it, had they been there, but his father laughed and let it go.

"Not worth Ameyumi's time," he said. Ameyumi was

the name of his bow, a family treasure, huge, perfectly balanced, made of many layers of compressed wood with intricate bindings.

They went stealthily toward the trees from which the sounds came. He remembered feeling it was a game, tiptoeing through the grass that was as tall as he was.

His father stopped, holding his breath, so Kazumaru knew something had startled him. He bent and picked him up and in that moment Kazumaru glimpsed the tengu playing Go beneath the trees, their wings, their beaked faces, their taloned hands.

Then his father was striding back to the place where they had found the fawn. He could feel his father's heart beating loud through his chest.

"Wait here," he said, placing his son in the trampled grass of the form. "Be like the deer's child. Don't move."

"Where are you going?"

"I am going to play Go," he replied, laughing again. "How often do you get the chance to play Go against tengu?"

Kazumaru didn't want him to. He had heard stories about tengu, mountain goblins, very clever, very cruel. But his father was afraid of nothing and always did exactly as he pleased.

The men found Shigetomo's body later that day. Kazumaru was not allowed to see it, but he heard the shocked whispers, and remembered the beaks, the claws as the tengu flew overhead. *They saw me*, he thought. *They know me.*

When they returned home, Sademasa reported that his older brother had been killed by wild tribes in the north, but Kazumaru knew, no matter who actually killed him, that he had died because he had played Go with the tengu and lost.

※

The news of his father's death plunged Kazumaru's mother into a grief so extreme, everyone feared she could not survive it. Sademasa pleaded with her to marry him in his brother's place, saying he would bring Kazumaru up as his own son, even swearing an oath on a sacred ox-headed talisman.

"Both of you remind me of him all the time," she said. "No, I must cut my hair and become a nun, as far away from Kumayama as possible." As soon as the winter was over, she left, with hardly a word of farewell, beyond telling Kazumaru to obey his uncle.

The family held a small parcel of land, confirmed by Lord Kiyoyori, on the side of the mountain known as Kumayama. It was made up of steep crags and deep, sunless valleys, where a few rice paddies had been carved out on either side of the rivers that tumbled from the mountain between forests of cypress and cryptomeria, full of bears, wolves, serow and deer, and boars, and groves of bamboo, home to quail and pheasants. It was seven days' journey east of the capital and four days in the other direction from the Miboshi stronghold of Minatogura.

As the years went by, it became apparent that Sademasa was not going to keep his oath. He grew accustomed to being the Kumayama lord and was reluctant to give it up. Power, along with unease at his own faithlessness, unleashed his brutal nature. He treated his nephew harshly, under the pretext of turning him into a warrior. Before he was twelve years old, Kazumaru realized that each day he lived brought his uncle fresh disappointment that he was not dead.

Some of Sademasa's warriors, in particular one Naganori, whose son was a year older than Kazumaru, were saddened by the harsh treatment of their former lord's son. Others such as Nobuto admired Sademasa for his ruthlessness. The rest shrugged their shoulders, especially after Sademasa married and had children of his own, thinking that it made no difference, as Kazumaru would probably never be allowed to grow up, let alone inherit the estate. Most of them were surprised that he survived his brutalizing childhood and even flourished in some ways, for he practiced obsessively with the bow and from his rages came a superhuman strength. At twelve years he suddenly grew tall, and soon after could string and draw a bow like a grown man. But he was as shy and fierce as a young wolf. Only Naganori's son, who received the name Nagatomo in his coming-of-age ceremony, was in any way a friend.

He was the only person to whom Kazumaru said goodbye when, in the autumn of his sixteenth year, his uncle announced he was taking him hunting in the mountains.

"If I don't come back, you'll know he has killed me," Kazumaru said. "Next year I come of age, but he will never step aside for me. He has grown too fond of being the lord of Kumayama. He intends to get rid of me in the forest."

"I wish I could come with you," Nagatomo said. "But your uncle has expressly forbidden it."

"That proves I am right," Kazumaru replied. "But even if he doesn't kill me I will not be coming back. There's nothing for me here. I've only the vaguest memories of what it was like before. I remember not being afraid all the time, being loved and admired. Sometimes I daydream about what might have happened if my father had not died, if my mother had not left, if more of the men were loyal to me . . . but that's the way it turned out. Don't grieve for me. I can't go on living in this way. I pray every day to escape somehow—if the only way is through death, so be it."

2

KAZUMARU/SHIKANOKO

The summer storms had abated and every day the stain of red leaves descended farther from the peaks. That year's fawns were almost full grown but still followed their mothers through the shade-dappled forest.

There was a famous old stag with a fine set of antlers that Sademasa had long desired, but the creature was cunning and cautious and never allowed itself to be encircled. This would be the year, Sademasa declared, that the stag would surrender to him.

He took his nephew, his favorite retainer, Nobuto, and one other man. They went on foot, for the terrain was too rough even for the sure-footed horses that grazed on the lower slopes of Kumayama. They lived like wild men, gathering nuts and berries, shooting pheasants and setting traps for hares, every day going farther into the pathless forest, now and then catching glimpses of their prey, then losing it again until they came upon its tracks in the soft earth or its brown compact scat. Kazumaru expected his uncle to grow impatient, but instead Sademasa became almost jovial, as though he were about to be relieved of a burden he had carried for a long time. At night the men told ghost stories about tengu and mountain sorcerers, and all the ways young boys had disappeared. Kazumaru swore he would not let himself be killed along with the stag. He hardly dared sleep but sometimes fell into a kind of waking dream and heard the clack of Go stones and saw the eagle eyes of tengu turned toward him.

They came one afternoon to the summit of a steep crag and the stag stood before them, its antlers gleaming in the western rays of the sun. Its flanks were heaving with the effort of the climb. The men were panting. There was a moment of stillness. Sademasa and Kazumaru both had their bows drawn. The other two men stood with knives ready. Sademasa gestured to Kazumaru to move around to the left, and drew his bow. Kazumaru was about to draw his, seeing where he would aim, right at the heart. The stag looked at him, its eyes wide with exertion and fear. Then its gaze flickered toward Sademasa and Kazumaru followed it. In that instant he saw his uncle's bow was aimed not at the stag but at him. Then the stag was leaping straight at him in its desperate lunge to escape. The arrow flew, the stag collided with Kazumaru and sent him crashing down with it into the valley below.

The animal broke his fall. As they both lay unmoving, winded, he could feel the frantic beat of its heart beneath him. He reached for the antlers and grasped them, then stood, fumbling for his knife. The deer was wounded, its legs broken. Its eyes watched him, unblinking. He prayed briefly and slit its throat, the hot blood pouring from it as its life slipped away.

Thick bushes hid him from the men above. He could hear their shouts but made no sound in response. He wondered if his uncle's desire for the antlers would be so great that he would follow him down the cliff, but the only way was to jump or fall. When silence returned he dragged the stag as far as he could, finding a small hollow under a bank filled with dry leaves. He lay down with the dead beast in his arms, slaking his thirst in its blood, reliving the moment on the cliff. It would have been easy to tell himself it was an accident, but it seemed important to face the truth. His uncle had aimed at him, but the stag had taken the arrow. It had saved his life. And then he felt again his own fall, the astonishment of flight, his hand gripping the bow as if it would hold him up, too young to believe in his own mortality yet expecting incredulously to die.

All night he sensed wild animals circling, drawn by the smell of blood. He heard the pad of their feet, the rustling of leaves. The sky was ablaze with stars, the River of Heaven pouring light.

At dawn the stag had cooled. He moved it into the clearing and set about skinning it, carefully cutting out the brainpan and the antlers, regretful for the way life had vanished so quickly from the eyes and face, wishing it could be restored, all the time filled with gratitude.

He found flintlike stones and spent the morning scraping the skin clean. The sun came around the valley and for a few hours it was hot. In the early afternoon he carved several strips of meat from the haunches, thin so they could dry quickly, and threaded them on a shaft cut from an oak tree, placing leaves between them. He left the rest of the carcass for the foxes and wolves and began to walk toward the north.

Mostly he walked all night; the moon was waxing toward full, bringing the first frosts. He slept for brief periods in the middle of the day, after softening the deer hide with water or his own urine and spreading it out to dry. He saw no one, but on the third day he became aware an animal was tracking him. He heard the pad and rustle of its tread and saw the green gleam of its eyes. Several times he set an arrow to the bowstring, but then the eyes vanished and he did not shoot. He did not want to lose an arrow in the dark.

It seemed to be guiding him or, he reflected uneasily, herding him. From time to time he thought it had gone, but at nightfall it always returned. Once he caught a glimpse of it and knew from its size and color that it was a wolf, drawn by the scent of the deerskin and the meat. He and his uncle had pursued the stag to the point of exhaustion and now the wolf was doing the same to him. It was driving him farther and farther into the forest, and when he was exhausted and weakened by hunger it would spring at his throat. He tried to outwit it, pretending to sleep then rising soundlessly, changing direction, but it seemed aware of his intentions even before he was. He saw its green eyes shining in his path.

One morning at dawn he stopped beside a stream that flowed through an upland clearing from a spring farther up the mountain. He had eaten the last of the dried meat a day ago. A path had been worn through the grass and there were tracks at the water's edge. He saw that animals came to drink there: deer, foxes, wolves. He slaked his own thirst warily, gulping quickly from cupped hands. Then he hid upwind with arrow drawn.

He must have dozed off, for a sudden movement woke him. He thought he was dreaming. Two animals appeared walking awkwardly side by side, their heads turned toward each other. They were carrying something between them, in their mouths. They walked strangely, as though they were not quite alive. Their heads were lacquered skulls, their teeth sharp and glistening, their eyes bright shards of lapis lazuli. Their skins did not cover flesh but seemed to be packed with straw and twigs. He caught their smell of smoke and putrefaction; his stomach heaved and his guts twisted.

As they came closer he saw the object they carried in their mouths was a two-handled water jar. They stood in the pool and lowered the jug into the stream. When it had filled they turned and walked back along the path, staggering a little and spilling water as they went.

Kazumaru followed them as though in a dream, without questioning but not without fear. He could hear the thump of his blood in his skull and chest. He knew he was approaching the lair of a mountain sorcerer, just as his uncle's men had described. He wanted to flee, yet he was driven forward not only by his own curiosity and hunger but also by the wolf, which now padded openly behind him.

He passed a rock that looked a little like a bear and then a tree stump with two jagged branches like a hare's ears. Closer to a small hut, which stood in the shelter of a paulownia tree, the forms became more lifelike and precise: statues carved from wood and stone, some with the same lacquered skulls, some draped in skins or decorated with antlers; owls, eagles, and cranes with feathers; bats with leathery wings.

The hut's roof was thatched with bones, its walls covered with skins. A strong smell of urine came from a large bucket by the door. One detached part of his mind thought, *He must use it for tanning hides*, just as his own urine had softened the stag's skin. Two fox cubs, real, were snarling at each other over a dead rabbit. The wolf sat on its haunches, panting slightly. The two beasts Kazumaru had been following stopped in front of the hut and whined. After a few seconds the sorcerer emerged. He took the jug from their mouths and made a gesture for them to sit as if they were dogs. His skin was tanned like leather, his hair long, his beard wispy, both deepest black with no sign of gray. He seemed both old and young. His movements were as deft and free of thought as an animal's, but his voice when he addressed Kazumaru was human.

"Welcome home. So, you have come back to Shisoku?"

"Have I been here before?" Kazumaru said. Behind him the wolf howled.

"In this life or another."

And maybe he had. Who knew where the soul voyaged while the body slept? Perhaps it had the strange familiarity of dreams.

"Did you bring the shoulder blades?" the man called Shisoku asked abruptly.

"No, I—" Kazumaru began, but the sorcerer cut him off.

"Never mind. No doubt they'll turn up one day. Give me the antlers. We still have time."

"Time for what?"

"To make you the deer's child. That's why you came."

"What does that mean?"

"Your life is not your own. You will die to one life and rise to another, to become what you are meant to be."

He turned at that moment and tried to run, but the sorcerer spoke words in a language he did not know and then said, "You will stay!" and the words were like bars closing around him. He felt bony hands grasp his forearms, though the sorcerer stood some distance from him. Shisoku stepped slowly backward and Kazumaru was drawn into the hut.

❋

He was not sure if he was in a dwelling, a workshop, or a shrine. There were scents of lacquer, camphor, and incense, not quite masking the stench of dead things. In the hearth a fire blazed under an iron pot in which bubbled an unrecognizable brew. Carving tools and paintbrushes lay on a smoke-blackened bench. The floor was of packed earth, but at one end, in front of a sort of altar, rugs and cushions had been spread, surrounded by glittering lamps and candles. Carved figures of deities, all with lacquered and painted faces, stood on and around the altar, and on the wall hung many masks and animal heads, together with their skins. He could see at least two human skulls. He realized he had arrived at one of those places where the worlds mingle, like the place that had haunted his childhood dreams, where his father met the tengu. He began to tremble, but there was no escape. Outside, the hut was surrounded by animals, both real and counterfeit. Inside was the sorcerer.

Without knowing how it happened he was lying before the altar, naked, covered only by the deer skin. He looked up at Shisoku with the same eyes as the stag, widened and resigned in the face of death. Shisoku gave him a drink of mushrooms and pine needles, mixed with lacquer and cinnabar, which would ordinarily kill a man but put Kazumaru into a deep trance. Time stopped.

Kazumaru watched him take the antlers and the half-moon-shaped brainpan and begin to create a mask, chanting as he worked, some mysterious sutra that Kazumaru had never heard before. Slowly day turned to night. Outside, the animals stirred and cried out. It seemed to Kazumaru that a woman lay next to him. He was filled with fear, for he had never been with a woman, had avoided the knowing glances of the maids at Kumayama, suspicious of all they seemed to offer, wary of the ways humans hurt each other. But she led him on to embrace her, many times that night and the following ones, his cries mingling with the animals'. He knew his body, his strength, his maleness,

17

were being used for purposes he did not understand, against his will. Nevertheless his own lust rose to meet hers.

In the day he lay unable to move and watched Shisoku as he painted the mask with layer upon layer of lacquer and the red and white fluids produced by the lovers. He dried each layer by passing it through smoke from the incense, chanting a different spell each time. He made lips and a tongue from cured leather painted with cinnabar, carved out hollows for the eyes and fringed them with black lashes cut from the woman's hair. He polished the antlers until they shone like obsidian. The moon waxed to full and waned into nothingness. When it was next half-grown the mask was finished.

Shisoku fitted it to Kazumaru's face. It clung to his features like a glove to a hand. He felt rush through him the strength of the stag and all the ancient wisdom of the forest. The woman came to him one last time. His cries echoed like the stag in autumn. She held him tenderly and whispered, "Now your name is Shikanoko, the deer's child." A distant memory came to him—a fawn, his father's voice—and he knew he would never take another name. Then he fell into a deep sleep. When he awoke he was clothed again, the woman had gone, and the stag's mask lay in a seven-layered brocade bag on the altar. It did not seem possible that it should fit in a bag that size, but it was one more aspect of the spells that Shisoku had cast on it.

❋

Shisoku practiced a kind of haphazard, offhand magic. He made a vague gesture toward the fire, which sprang into life seven times out of ten and the other three sulked in disobedience. The live foxes and wolves occasionally appeared when he summoned them but more often went on with their wild lives as if the sorcerer were not living among them. Sometimes the artificial animals did what was expected of them, fetched water in the jug, gathered firewood, but shards of pottery at the water's edge indicated how many times they had failed. Shikanoko collected firewood himself and as winter wore on went out hunting to feed them both. He made new arrows and fletched them with eagle's feathers, but though he spotted and followed many deer he never killed one again.

Shisoku ate very little, but spent his days skinning and plucking, preserving skins and plumage with camphor and rue, boiling up skulls and bones to get rid of every last trace of flesh. Then painstakingly he re-created the dead animals as though he were some kind of creator spirit, stuffing the skins with clay and straw, building frames of bamboo and cord to hold the skeleton together. His creations stood in rows under the eaves, the snow drifting across them. For many weeks the frost preserved them, but when spring came insects returned, too. Eggs hatched into grubs and most of the crawling mass had to be burned. One or two survived, by luck, skill, or magic, and came to life and joined Shisoku's collection.

The snows melted high in the mountains and the stream flooded almost up to the door of the hut. After it receded, grass and wildflowers covered the clearing. Every night Shisoku placed the mask on Shikanoko's face and taught him the movements of the deer dance.

"This dance unlocks the secrets of the forest and releases its blessings. It is a powerful link between the three worlds of animals, humans, and spirits. When you have mastered the dance you will gain knowledge through the mask. You will know all the events of the world, you will see the future in dreams, and all your wishes will be granted."

The movements awakened something in him that he both craved and feared, but he thought it was probably unreliable like all Shisoku's magic and he only partly believed it.

☀

Just after the full moon of the equinox a band of ten horsemen came into the clearing.

"It is the King of the Mountain, Akuzenji," Shisoku said. He did not seem alarmed.

Shikanoko took up his bow anyway. He was sure the woman who rode with them was the one who had accompanied him through his initiation and the creation of the mask, but she gave no sign of recognizing him. He was filled with intense curiosity about her and sudden shyness in her presence. He wanted to ask her a hundred questions but could not find the words for one.

Akuzenji dismounted and added a stream of urine to Shisoku's bucket, saying, "My contribution to your work. I'm sure it has magic properties." He was a broad, squat man with tangled hair and beard. He wore a shabby corselet of leather plates laced with faded green cords and carried a huge sword—both looked as if they had been stolen from some ambushed warrior. He said to Shisoku, "I've just come to check you are keeping safe the treasure I entrusted to you."

"I placed it under a binding spell," Shisoku replied. "Shall I release it to you?"

"Not yet. Business is good, I've no need of it. But I'd like to take a look at it."

Shisoku bowed in his offhand way and waved him toward the hut. He followed Akuzenji inside while the other men dismounted, urinated into the bucket in turn, and squatted down by the fire. After a while Akuzenji came out, a smile of satisfaction on his face, and sauntered toward Shikanoko.

"And who might you be?"

"I was Kumayama no Kazumaru, but now I am Shikanoko."

"The boy who fell off the mountain last year? You were believed to be dead."

"I came here and the sorcerer looked after me."

"Did he?" Akuzenji's shrewd black eyes took in the bow and the fletched arrows. "I don't suppose your uncle will pay a ransom for you, will he?"

"He would be more likely to pay for confirmation of my death," Shikanoko said, wondering if he had just invited the King of the Mountain to kill him.

"What about Lord Kiyoyori? He'd be your liege lord, wouldn't he? Would he pay anything for you?"

"I don't suppose so," Shikanoko replied. "What use would I be to him?"

"A pawn has many uses, but only if it is alive," the woman said.

It was her—he recognized her voice. It roused both anger and fear in him, at the way she and Shisoku had used him, but he also felt a pang of longing for that deep intimacy when their bodies had been joined as one and an object of beauty and magic had been created.

Akuzenji frowned and scratched his head, studying Shikanoko with a probing look. "How old are you?" he said.

"I turned sixteen in the new year."

"Can you use that bow?"

"I can, but I will not kill deer."

"But will you kill men?"

"I have no objection to killing men," he replied.

"Then I will tie up your hair; you can swear allegiance to me, and come with us."

Shikanoko sought Shisoku's eyes. Was he to go or stay? The sorcerer did not return his gaze.

It was not the coming-of-age ceremony he had expected: he had thought he would kneel before the Kuromori lord, Kiyoyori, in the presence of his uncle and all their warriors. Instead there was the spring clearing, the wood smoke in his eyes, the rough lord who took him into his service, the animals half living and half dead. When it was done he placed some of the arrows in his quiver, tied the rest in a bundle, and took up his bow. Shisoku went into the hut, came out with the seven-layered bag containing the mask, and gave it to Shikanoko.

The woman unloaded sacks of grain, rice, millet, and bean paste from one of the horses and took them into the hut. The men were gathering up any usable skins and feathers. Akuzenji eyed the seven-layered bag.

"What's that?"

Shisoku gave him no answer.

"Show me," Akuzenji demanded, and, after a moment's pause, Shikanoko drew the mask from the bag and held it up.

Akuzenji took a step back, silenced, angry. When he could speak, he said, "This is the sort of thing I've always wanted from you. When am I going to get it? For years I've been begging you. I want a skull of divination to be my oracle, to tell me all things. You know the secret techniques and rituals; why do you keep denying me?"

"It is not me who denies you," the sorcerer muttered, but Akuzenji was in full flow.

"I have brought you many skulls. Surely no one has brought you as many. What did the boy bring you? Why did you favor him?"

"He came at the right time," Shisoku said. "I'm sorry."

"So when is the right time?"

"It is when the time is right. The skulls you bring are worthless—dull peasants or desperate criminals or warriors steeped in blood. Bring me a wise man or a shrewd minister, an ascetic or a great king."

"Is that what the boy brought you?" Akuzenji was incredulous. "How?"

"He is Shikanoko, the deer's child. What he brought was for him alone."

Akuzenji stuck out his lower lip and narrowed his eyes. "What about Kiyoyori's skull? What if I brought that?"

"Kiyoyori is undoubtedly a great man," Shisoku replied. "But he is not going to let you take his head."

The woman spoke again, "Kiyoyori's skull is not for you, Akuzenji. If you try for it you will lose your own."

She and Shisoku exchanged a slight glance, a fleeting smile, making Shikanoko shiver as he caught a glimpse of the secret worlds they moved in, worlds that he was now part of.

He knelt in thanks before the sorcerer, who smiled slightly and brushed him away.

He looked back as they rode off. One of the wolves had approached the hut and the sorcerer stood with his hand on its head.

The rider next to him laughed. "Old Four Legs! Did you learn any useful tricks from him?"

He waggled four fingers in Shikanoko's face. "Did he turn you into a four legs, too?"

There was a flash of lightning, a sudden crack of thunder. A pine tree in their path split in half, smoking. The horses reared and plunged to the side, nearly unseating them.

"Make sure you are far away before you speak ill of the sorcerer," the woman said quietly.

The man looked chastened and Shikanoko was glad the magic had for once been effective. He rode behind the woman, knowing that he had indeed embraced her many times, that together they had made the mask, but at the same time not understanding how that was possible. How would she make such a journey night after night? Did she have magic powers or had he lain with a spirit woman, summoned by Shisoku? Had he lain with a demon?

3

KIYOYORI

Lord Kiyoyori was twenty-eight years of age, the time when men approach the height of their physical and mental powers. He was descended from the Kakizuki family, who took their name from the persimmon-colored moon of autumn. Their founder was the son of an emperor who renounced his imperial rank and took an ordinary surname and whose sons and grandsons prospered, becoming skillful statesmen, gifted poets, and fine warriors, while his granddaughters became wives and mothers of emperors.

Though Kiyoyori's family were younger sons of younger sons and so not of the highest rank or importance, his father, Kiyomasa, had always had the deepest respect for his name and had done his utmost to preserve it. He had endeavored to bring his sons up as perfect warriors, experts with horse, bow, and sword, and unquestioningly obedient to their father's will.

Kiyomasa frequently visited the capital, Miyako, and kept himself fully abreast of all the politics and intrigues of the court. The Kakizuki family held many important posts but so did their rivals, the Miboshi, also of imperial descent. Kiyoyori's grandmother had been a Miboshi, for in more peaceful times the two great families had often intermarried. But recently relations between them had been less cordial.

For years the Miboshi had been fighting the Emperor's battles in the east and north of the Eight Islands, bringing clans under their control and subduing various barbaric tribes. Their lord, Aritomo, had established himself in Minatogura in the east, but many of his warriors were turning up in Miyako, expecting rewards for their services, including court positions, new ranks, and land.

There were not enough of any of these to go around.

Warrior families, aware of intrigues in the Emperor's court and in the government, were striving among one another for position and influence. Kiyomasa tried to arrange advantageous marriages for his sons, and at seventeen Kiyoyori had been married to a woman from the domain of Maruyama in the west, whose father was a counselor in the Kakizuki government. The marriage had worked out well, a child was born, and then another, but this second one took the life of her mother, and then slipped away after her, across the river of death, leaving Kiyoyori grief stricken. He had loved her deeply and felt he would never recover from her loss. His only consolation was their first child, a daughter, whose pet name was Hina.

The younger brother, Masachika, had also made a desirable marriage, to the daughter of a neighbor who owned an extensive and productive estate known as Matsutani, or Pine Valley. It was all destined for Lord Matsutani's son, but the day after his sister's marriage, on the journey home, the young man had attempted to swim his horse across the swollen river and had been swept away and drowned. There were no other heirs and it seemed everything would go to Masachika's new wife. Masachika himself assumed his father-in-law would adopt him, giving him a far greater and richer estate than his older brother's.

However, his father had other plans, which he announced a few months after the death of Kiyoyori's wife. Kiyoyori was twenty-one, Masachika nineteen. The brothers were summoned to a meeting in one of the secret rooms in the house at Kuromori, a fortified residence built mainly of wood in an inaccessible position on a mountainside surrounded by the Darkwood from which they took their name. It had several hidden rooms; this one faced south and was the warmest. Perhaps for this reason it had been taken over by a man of indeterminate age and unremarkable appearance who had the reputation of being a great scholar. He certainly spent a lot of time reading and the room was filled with his scrolls and manuscripts, which he collected from the eight corners of Heaven and which were in many languages. He had a monkish sort of name, Sesshin, and could sometimes be heard chanting. Nobody took much notice of him. Kiyoyori found his presence vaguely reassuring, like that of an old dog.

It was a showery autumn day, rain sweeping across the valley. The shutters were closed, the room dim even though it was not yet mid-afternoon. The thought of winter approaching filled Kiyoyori with gloom. He could not shake off the sadness that had fallen on him since his wife died.

He had been outside the stables when his father sent for him. He wanted to start teaching Hina to ride and had been trying out a suitable pony, with the help of most of the children of the estate. For some time he had feared that his father was going to announce he had found him another bride. Naturally he would have to marry and produce an heir, but at the moment he felt more inclined to cut his hair and become a monk. Only Hina kept him from such a decision. He came to the meeting with some apprehension, which increased as they sat waiting for his brother. The shutters rattled as gusts of wind shook them and rain beat heavily on the roof. His father kept giving impatient glances up from under his eyebrows and sighing heavily.

Eventually Masachika appeared, full of excuses for his tardiness. He had an air of expectation, as though all his desires were at last to be confirmed.

Their father began to speak. "I know you believe as I do that our most important aim must be the survival and increase in influence and power of our family. I believe we are approaching very dangerous times. There have been many evil omens in the capital, and diviners predict warfare and chaos. Our estate is too small to support sufficient warriors to give us much influence. Now fate has given us the opportunity to merge with Matsutani."

Masachika nodded and a faint smile appeared on his well-shaped mouth.

"But I cannot dispossess my eldest son," their father continued, "for whom I have such a high regard, and to give the greater estate to the younger son is asking for conflict. Therefore, I have decided that you, Masachika, will put aside your wife and go to our Miboshi relatives in Minatogura. My cousin has one daughter only and has agreed to adopt you as his son. Kiyoyori will marry your former wife and will inherit both estates. Her father is in complete agreement. This way, if war does erupt between Kakizuki and Miboshi, whichever side prevails, one of my sons will be among the victors."

For a few moments neither of them spoke. Then Masachika said, trying to control himself, "I am to give my wife to my brother? I am to lose her and Matsutani?"

"There is no need to be so drastic, Father," Kiyoyori said. "Let my brother keep his wife. I will renounce my claim to both estates. I wish to retire from the world—"

"Don't be a fool," his father snapped. "You are my eldest son and heir. Do you think I would allow you to humiliate yourself and become a monk? A man does not flee from the world. He bears up under its sorrows and does his duty. Yours is to me and your family. After all, you have your daughter to consider."

Kiyoyori tried then and later to dissuade his father from making the two brothers enemies in such an irretrievable manner. He dared to admonish him, citing many instances from classical literature where brothers had destroyed each other and whole kingdoms, but Kiyomasa would not brook any contradiction. Masachika had to hide his rage and resentment and Kiyoyori his reluctance, and both had to submit.

Later, after Masachika had left for Minatogura, his father said to Kiyoyori, "I believe you will improve the land and defend it. Masachika wanted only to enjoy it. It would have been swiftly taken from him. Old Matsutani knows that, which is why he agreed with me. Besides, the men prefer you and you know how to treat them."

✳

It was a time of troubles and opportunities. In the capital the Emperor was weak, his sons rivals. His brother-in-law, the Prince Abbot at Ryusonji, was regent in all but name. He favored the Emperor's younger son and carried on endless intrigues against the Crown Prince.

In the provinces the Kakizuki extended their power in the west and the Miboshi in the east while both strove for influence in the capital. Warlords fought constant skirmishes, seeking always to increase their land. More land meant more warriors, who in turn could be used to gain more land. Retainers were persuaded to swear undying loyalty, but they expected much in return. If they felt badly treated or overlooked, their loyalty was eroded; they could be seduced away to another warlord's service, someone who appreciated them and offered greater rewards.

✳

Kiyoyori was all too aware that no one had asked Tama, the woman who had been Masachika's wife and was now his, for her consent or even her opinion. She was as obedient to her father as her husbands were to theirs. Kiyoyori waited several weeks to make sure she was not pregnant, and when he did approach her he felt as shy and awkward as an adolescent. She responded dutifully but without any real passion, and while he knew he could not blame her for this, it still wounded his pride. He felt his younger brother would always lie between them. Even his delight and gratitude when she gave birth to a son could not break down the barriers between them. She nursed the baby herself, used this as an excuse to keep him away, and from then on they slept apart. Kiyoyori continued to feel obscurely guilty about her and treated her with excessive courtesy, masking the absence of real warmth and intimacy. It was for her sake that he moved to Matsutani, for she loved her childhood home and put all her energies into making the residence more beautiful and the estate more productive than ever. Kiyoyori took his horses and his dogs and somehow the old scholar went with them, along with all his books. Matsutani was certainly more comfortable and more convenient, but no one ever referred to its owner as anything other than the Kuromori lord. The Darkwood was his true home.

In the following years both fathers left this world to cross the Three-Streamed River for that place of underground springs and caves where they would face the judges of Hell. Kiyoyori was, as his father had predicted, a good leader of men, as well as being both courageous and astute. He was quick to anger and impulsive, acting swiftly on instinct, but his instincts were usually correct and his anger, together with a degree of ruthlessness, meant he was feared as well as admired. His fame spread. He fought several small but well-planned skirmishes that subdued his neighbors and rivals, not only holding on to his own lands but also extending them. The twin estates of Kuromori and Matsutani seemed blessed. Some said it was karma due to good deeds in a former life; others that the estates must be protected by powerful magic and charms.

One dawn in the ninth month when he was walking toward the horse lines, for it was his custom to ride every morning with two or three retainers or young pages, Kiyoyori realized he did not have his whip. He must have left it somewhere in the residence. He thought of sending a groom back for it but, not being sure exactly where it was, decided it would be quicker to fetch it himself.

He stepped onto the wide veranda and pushed up the bamboo blind. The wooden shutters had already been opened, as the day promised to be fine and warm. There was someone in the room, one of the servants, he thought at first, but the person did not bow or glide respectfully away. Instead, whomever it was sat down cross-legged as if he planned to stay for a while and said, "There you are! I have been waiting for you."

"It would have been a long wait," Kiyoyori replied, ignoring the familiar tone. Eccentric old men could be allowed a few liberties. "On a beautiful day like this I might have ridden until midday."

"I knew you would return for this." The whip lay in the old scholar's wrinkled palm.

"Well, thank you, Master Sesshin." Kiyoyori stepped forward to take it, but without him quite seeing how, the whip switched sides and now lay on the other palm. All his senses came alert. He knelt in front of Sesshin, keeping his eyes fixed on his face. He realized he had hardly spared the old fellow a glance in all the years they had lived under the same roof. Indeed, he had averted his eyes and made efforts not to notice him, finding his slovenly appearance vaguely affronting and his body odor disconcerting. The thought came to him that maybe the old man had kept himself concealed in some way and now for the first time he was allowing Kiyoyori to see him.

The skin was like ancient silk, drawn taut over the bones. The eyes returned the lord's gaze guilelessly, but they held an unfathomable depth. They had looked on worlds he had not even dreamed of and into mysteries he would never understand.

He spoke brusquely to hide his unease. "Do you have something to say to me? If you wanted to speak to me why did you not send a message?"

Sesshin laughed, a dry, crackling noise like old wood burning. "You would have put me off and gone out today, and then it would have been too late."

"What do you mean?"

"There is a bandit, Akuzenji. He calls himself the King of the Mountain."

"I know who Akuzenji is. I have no quarrel with him.

As long as he stays on the mountain, does not extract excessive amounts from merchants, and deals with his rivals swiftly he is causing me no harm. I don't have enough men to place guards on the whole length of the North Mountain Road. Let Akuzenji do my work for me; I don't have to pay him."

"He is going to demand a high price from you. He has taken a fancy to your skull."

Kiyoyori laughed. The idea that a bandit would dare to attack him, the Kuromori lord, amused him. "Give me my whip and I'll be on my way."

"Well, if you must ignore my warning, take extra men and be on your guard. Or tonight your head will be in a pot, the flesh boiling from it, and before the next moon your brother will be back in Matsutani and your children will be dead."

"Is my brother plotting with Akuzenji? Is that what you are trying to tell me?"

"*Plotting* is not perhaps quite the right word. Akuzenji has no personal enmity toward you. He simply wants the skull of a great man. He is an undiscerning fellow. He boasts of every exploit before and after its achievement. He may never have seen you, but he knows you to be great because your fame spreads more widely every year. Your brother is an opportunist. He prays for your death before your son is grown so he may take back what he believes you stole from him."

"Akuzenji seeks the skull of a great man? For some kind of dark magic?"

"I believe so," the old man said.

"I should offer him yours!"

"Certainly my skull would be extremely powerful, as would all parts of me. Luckily for me, Akuzenji does not know of my existence, nor does anyone else. That is why, Lord Kiyoyori, it is in my interests to keep you alive."

"How do you know these things? Who are you?"

"Don't you wonder why you never thought to ask me before?"

"You have always been around ever since I was born," Kiyoyori said slowly. "You were part of the household like an old chest or a tree in the garden." He could have said, *like a dog*, but he realized the dogs died one after the other, at their allotted time, but the old man had lived on and on.

"Kuromori became my home when your grandfather was lord. We were friends. He arranged I should stay on after his death throughout your father's time. The place suited me, and Matsutani is even better; it's perfect for my studies and research. In return I have been able to perform certain rituals that have ensured the safety and prosperity of your domain."

"And I thought it was all due to my hard work and good management!"

"You have played your part. I would not have wasted my efforts on an inferior person. Spells can go only so far."

Kiyoyori said nothing for a few moments. Outside a kite was mewing, the wind soughed in the pine trees, a horse neighed impatiently from the stables.

Sesshin said, "You say you cannot afford to guard the

North Mountain Road, but if you removed Akuzenji and his bandits the merchants would pay you for their safe passage."

"Akuzenji is as cunning and elusive as a wolf," Kiyoyori replied, "but if he can be enticed by my skull I may take him by surprise."

"Wear armor under your hunting robe," Sesshin said. "And send someone as a decoy on your horse: Tachiyama no Enryo, for example."

"Enryo? Why do you name him?"

"He sends messages occasionally to your brother in Minatogura."

"Does he, now?" There was another short silence. "His wife is a great favorite of my wife. They have been friends since childhood." Was Tama also in touch with his brother, her first husband? Kiyoyori could feel fury building within him.

4

SHIKANOKO

Shika, as the bandits called him, was neither happy nor unhappy in the service of the King of the Mountain, in the high fastness that was Akuzenji's base. From time to time he wondered if this was to be the rest of his life or if he should return to Kumayama and confront his uncle. On the whole it seemed better to let everyone in his old life believe him to be dead.

He felt he was waiting every day to see what would happen to him. Akuzenji called himself King of the Mountain, just as pirates styled themselves Kings of the Sea, but in the eyes of most they were still pirates and Akuzenji no more than a bandit. Shika learned how he protected merchants and their goods on their way to the north and west, trading out of Kitakami and other seaports, where ships loaded with copper coins, iron, textiles, and medicines came from Silla and Shin, on the mainland. Akuzenji fought off other marauding bandits and made life safe for the woodsmen who cut trees on his mountain and sent the logs downstream to Lake Kasumi and then on to the capital. He had always been a superstitious man who liked to keep a number of shamans and sorcerers on the mountain and in the forest to consult about dreams and omens. Now he had become obsessed with obtaining a suitable skull for Shisoku's magic and had settled on the Kuromori lord.

He soon realized Shika could move as silently as a deer, with the same keen eyesight and hearing, and began to send him on scouting missions to the land around Matsutani. Shika came to know Lord Kiyoyori well: his favorite horse, a tall black stallion; his manner of riding; and the retainers and pages who accompanied him, to whom Shika assigned nicknames in his mind: Gripknees, Wobbly, Neversmile.

When he was not scouting he practiced archery, shooting endlessly at the straw targets, or made arrows from close-jointed bamboo, some with humming bulbs carved from magnolia wood. He fletched them with feathers he found in the forest or took from birds he hunted, eagles and cranes. He also carried out the countless chores that were laid on him as the youngest of Akuzenji's men, feeding and grooming the horses, including Akuzenji's white stallion, Nyorin, fetching water from the well and firewood from the forest, skinning and butchering dead beasts.

Only when he was alone and certain no one was watching did he take out the mask made from the deer's skull. He placed it over his face and tried to meditate. But what stirred within him was the ancient power of the forest, the stag's drive to mate and make children. There were many women in Akuzenji's fortress, but they already had husbands, lovers, or other protectors and favorites and were out of his reach. And then there was the one who had ridden with the bandit to the mountain sorcerer's hut, whose name he discovered was Lady Tora. Men lowered their voices when they spoke it and whispered about her among themselves. She had some power that terrified them, though they would never admit it. He knew the mask was powerful in the same way, but he had not yet learned to turn that power to his own advantage, and it left him disturbed and confused.

One warm, sultry evening he went deep into the forest and came upon a waterfall that fell white in the twilight into an opaque black pool in which was reflected the thin sickle of the new moon. Hot and restless, he took off his clothes, laid them on a rock with the brocade bag that held the mask, and plunged into the water. When he surfaced, shaking drops from his eyes, he saw some creature moving on the bank. He thought it was a deer coming to drink, but then he saw the long black hair and the pale face and realized it was a woman.

Lady Tora stood where he had left his clothes. She bent down and took the mask from the bag. She beckoned to him. He came naked out of the water, his skin wet and cool. She placed the mask on his face and kissed the cinnabar-colored lips. Beyond the rocks was a mossy bank and here they lay down together.

She was without a doubt the same woman who had come to him in the sorcerer's hut. She was using him for some purpose of her own, just as the sorcerer had used him to create the mask, but, as then, he had no will to resist. Skillfully she led him into the Great Bliss and together they heard the Lion's Roar. A sudden gust of wind drove spray over them, soaking them.

Then Tora took the mask off and kissed the real lips, the real eyes. "Now you must lie with no one, woman or man, until you wed the one who is meant for you."

"Will I never lie with you again?"

"No, our work together is finished."

She stroked his face tenderly as though he were her child. He was so unused to affection, he felt near tears.

"That was part of my mission, which one day you will understand," she said. "And it was the final ritual of the mask. Love is bound into its creation but so is lust, the force that drives the world to re-create itself, unconstrained by human rules."

"I understand nothing," he said.

"Use the mask carefully—it will bring you wisdom, but it will also lead you into danger. Practice abstinence and all the other disciplines our friend taught you in the forest. Subdue your body and mind so that when you meet her you will recognize her."

"Who is she?"

She did not answer him but told him to bathe himself again. The water was like ice on his body. When he came out she was gone.

The next morning just after daybreak Lady Tora rode out with Akuzenji and his men. She gave Shikanoko no sign of recognition, no glance, no smile. It was as if there were some other realm in which their meetings took place far removed from the conventions and relations of the everyday world. He wondered what Akuzenji's reaction would be if he knew; he was a violent man and Shikanoko had already seen the punishments he handed out for minor disobedience: an eye torn out, a hand amputated, brandings . . .

He shivered and kicked the brown mare he was riding. She still lagged behind the others. She was the oldest and slowest horse in the group, given to him because he was the newest arrival and the youngest. There was something about him that unsettled her, as horses were often alarmed by deer, and she tried many ways to rid herself of him, rubbing his legs against posts or walls, carrying him under low-hanging branches, taking him by surprise by shying or bucking. Her name was Risu. He had lost count of the number of times he had fallen off, a source of endless entertainment to the other men.

In her contrary way Risu had formed a bond of affection with her previous rider, a lanky man called Gozaemon, and whickered after him as he cantered ahead on the sturdy dark bay horse to which he had been promoted. Now she swung her head back and tried to bite Shika's foot.

Akuzenji was leading his men down the forest-covered slope toward the trail through the valley where Lord Kiyoyori rode every morning. The rest of the group were some way ahead, out of sight. Risu lifted her head and neighed as Gozaemon came trotting back.

"Hurry up," he said. "Lord Akuzenji wants you to kill someone." He grabbed Risu's rein and led her alongside his horse. She moved faster than she had all morning.

Akuzenji and his men had concealed themselves in a grove of bamboo on a rocky outcrop above the trail that ran between the forest and the cultivated fields. The rice had been cut and was hanging in sheaves to dry. Farmers were already at work, spreading manure and mulch. Akuzenji beckoned to Shika and said, "Get off your horse and take up position. I want you to shoot him in the neck or the chest. Don't hit his head whatever you do."

They could hear the sound of horses approaching. At the same time Shika became aware of a woman calling in the distance. She was running across the rice field, shouting and waving both arms. She looked awkward, almost comical, a noblewoman not used to running, her layered robes tangling round her legs. She slipped and fell sprawling into the manure.

Why was she running? He frowned, trying to work out what was going on.

The riders, a small group, not wearing armor, swept into view, the black stallion in the lead.

"Now," Akuzenji breathed. "Shoot him!"

"Shoot who?"

"The Kuromori lord! On the black!"

"That is not the Kuromori lord," Shika said, lowering

his bow slightly. "It's his horse, but it's not him." It was the man he called Neversmile.

"Shoot!" Akuzenji screamed in his ear.

Shika shrugged and obeyed. The arrow slammed into the unprotected neck. The blood sprayed in an arc of scarlet glistening in the first rays of sunlight. Dust rose in golden motes as the horse reared and the man fell.

The other riders halted and fell back as the bandits surged forward, Akuzenji in the lead. He had slid from his horse, seized the topknot of the fallen man with a yell of triumph, and was in the act of severing the head when there came a pounding of hooves, the shouting of men, and a host of armed warriors appeared. At their head was Lord Kiyoyori.

5

KIYOYORI

Kiyoyori was possessed by both rage and exhilaration as he surveyed the kneeling prisoners. All that day they had been held in the riding ground between the stables and the residence, under a chill wind, for the weather had changed suddenly, bringing the first intimation of winter.

The rage was against the disloyalty of his retainer, Enryo, who had taken his horse and died in his place. The exhilaration was for his survival, for the stallion's survival, for the painful deaths already suffered by some of those who had wanted his, and for the imminent execution of the rest.

Enryo's wife had revealed everything before she died: Akuzenji's scheme to take Kiyoyori's head, letters between his brother, Masachika, and Enryo, their desire to see Akuzenji's plan succeed and to seize the opportunity to regain the estate. His rage extended to his own wife, whom he had not yet questioned though she had been waiting for him, pale but dry-eyed, when he returned from the skirmish. She had expressed appropriate amazement at the audacity of the attack and equally suitable relief at her husband's survival, yet he felt she was lying. Of course it was not her fault that two old men had agreed to trade her between two brothers, but since she obviously had no deep feelings for him it was not unreasonable to suspect she might still harbor some for Masachika. She stood to benefit as much as anyone from Kiyoyori's death.

He thought for the thousandth time of his dead wife. If only Tsuki had lived!

If I had, you would not own Matsutani—would you really be willing to pay such a price?

He heard her teasing laugh and, looking across the riding ground, saw her standing in the front row among the prisoners. Surely it was her? The long black hair reaching to the ground, the slender form . . . he would recognize them anywhere even after eight years.

"I am sorry, lord," one of his men, Hachii Sadaike, said at his side. "She refuses to kneel; she has stood like that all day."

Oh, my beloved! You must be cold. One day in the frost and eight years in the grave.

"Lord Kiyoyori?" Sadaike said.

He came back to his senses. "Who is she?"

"A woman who rode with the bandits."

He looked at her and saw she was not Tsuki, though there was a resemblance. While he wondered at it, their eyes met. Once he had been close to a lightning strike and had felt all his hair stand on end. He experienced the same jolt now.

The woman bowed her head and fell to her knees before him. She would kneel for no one else but she would for him. An almost uncontrollable passion seized him, a desire stronger than he had ever known. He would have the whole band executed at once and then he would have her brought to him.

He had thought to devise some special punishment for Akuzenji, boiling him alive or sawing his head off slowly, to dissuade anyone else from daring to attack the Kuromori lord, but now his impatience would brook no delay. He was about to order Sadaike to take the woman aside and remove the heads of the rest, when the sky darkened and a shadow loomed over the riding ground. It swooped low over Kiyoyori's head and then rose to sit on the gable of the roof behind him. As he spun around to look at it, it began to call in a voice so ugly that everyone whose hands were not tied behind their backs immediately covered their ears.

Kiyoyori called for archers to shoot it down and his best bowmen came forward, eager to compete and win the lord's favor, but it was obviously an evil creature with supernatural powers, for their eyes were dazzled by the sun and their arrows clattered uselessly on the tiles. It was hard to perceive clearly: one moment it seemed dense and black, the next Kiyoyori thought he saw golden eyes like a monkey's above the needle-sharp beak. Its tail was long and sinuous like a snake and its legs were striped with gold, reflecting its eyes. It mocked them in a voice that was close to human, but inhuman, filling their souls with dread.

"Go to Master Sesshin," Kiyoyori instructed one of his pages. "Ask him what this creature means. Is it a sign that I must spare Akuzenji's life?"

He had spoken quietly, but the woman heard him.

"Do not send for the master," she said. "The bird has nothing to do with Akuzenji. Let Shikanoko kill it now at once."

Her voice thrilled him. He made a sign that she should approach him. "Who is Shikanoko?"

The woman walked toward him, then turned and called, "Shikanoko!"

Oh that she would call me like that! She will! She will!

"It was he who shot your decoy," she said to Kiyoyori.

"He would have killed me! I should put a bow in his hands now?"

"He spared your horse," she said gravely. "He is a good marksman."

"I suppose I cannot argue with that," Kiyoyori said, elation sweeping through him at her proximity.

The boy came forward, a young man on the cusp of adulthood. Fairly tall, thin, brown-skinned, he moved, despite his cramped limbs, with spare grace, like an animal. Kiyoyori studied him with narrowed eyes. He did not look like a bandit. He was surely a warrior's son; perhaps he had been kidnapped. If he could kill the bird he would be spared and Kiyoyori would find out who he was and restore him to his family or take him into his service. If he failed he would die along with the rest of them, which would serve him right for keeping such bad company.

"Give him his bow and arrows," he ordered.

He could tell his men did not like this command, nor did they relish the likelihood of being shown up by a stripling. There was a short delay while the bow and quiver were located among the piles of weapons that had been taken from the bandits and then they waited for Shikanoko to restring the bow. The bird called gratingly all the while, swinging its head from side to side and peering down with golden eyes, seeming to laugh in greater derision as Shikanoko drew the bow back, squinting against the sun. He lowered it as if the mocking intimidated him.

He will die tonight, Kiyoyori vowed.

Shikanoko whispered in the woman's ear.

"Something else was taken from him," she said to Kiyoyori. "It must be returned to him before he can shoot. A seven-layered brocade bag containing a mask."

"Find it," Kiyoyori commanded, barely able to control his impatience.

One of his men produced the bag a little shamefacedly.

The boy received it without speaking, his demeanor relaxing noticeably as he felt the contents of the bag.

"Tell him to show me what's inside," Kiyoyori said to the woman. He liked the idea of speaking through her as though the boy were a barbarian who needed an interpreter, as though he bound both of them closer to him by this means.

She said, "Show the lord."

Shikanoko drew out the mask and held it in both hands toward Kiyoyori, who gasped without meaning to at the almost living power of the face, the dark lashes over the eye sockets, the reddish lips and tongue. He saw the brainpan from which it had been formed and was conscious suddenly of his own skull, so hard yet so fragile. The mask seemed to float between woman and boy like an infant. He realized they had both taken part in its creation and jealousy flooded through him. The woman's eyes met his and he knew it was for this that Akuzenji had wanted his head, to turn it into a magic object of power.

He gestured upward with his head and Shika put the mask away, giving the bag to the woman to hold. The bird had fallen silent, peering down at them. Now it launched itself into flight, but it was too late. The arrow sped true from the bow, humming as it went. Its sound merged into the bird's cry of despair as it pierced the heart. Blood burst from the wound, falling in sizzling drops. Then the creature plunged headfirst to the ground.

"Bring it to Master Sesshin," Kiyoyori said. "He will know what it is."

❋

Even the most hardened warriors were reluctant to touch it, so Shikanoko, after drawing out the arrow and returning it to his quiver, wrapped it in the woman's shawl and carried it in both hands into the residence. Kiyoyori led the way to Sesshin's room. It was the first time he had been in it since the move to Matsutani, and the differing scents of old books, ink, lamp oil, and some sort of incense made his senses reel even more.

"It is a werehawk," Sesshin said, after inspecting it carefully. "How strange that it should come here now."

"What does it mean?" Kiyoyori demanded.

"I shall have to practice some divination to find out." The old scholar looked slightly perturbed. "What a mysterious coincidence of events. I knew something was awry, but I thought it affected only you. Now I fear there are wider forces converging, with far-reaching consequences."

He fell silent, gazing on the dead bird.

Kiyoyori felt suddenly weary. It seemed like days ago that he had returned for his whip. He wanted above all to lie down with this woman and wipe out the reproaches of the dead.

From outside came the sound of heads falling one by one as the bandits were executed. Most of them were resigned to their fate, not unexpected given their calling, and died quietly, some speaking the name of the Enlightened One, but a few struggled and cursed, wept and pleaded. It was a pitiful sound.

Shikanoko quivered at each sword blow, tears in his eyes. The woman remained calm, watching Sesshin carefully.

A great yell of defiance that could only be Akuzenji echoed like a thunderbolt. Shikanoko gasped as if he were about to sob.

"Lord Kiyoyori may leave now," the old man said. "And the woman had better take this boy away before he faints." His tone was dismissive and he hardly looked at

Shika, continuing to stare at the dead werehawk, a frown creasing his brow.

"We will stay with you," said the woman.

Kiyoyori and Sesshin spoke together. "That will not be necessary."

"I think you will find it is," she replied. "Please leave, lord." She looked from one to the other, though only Kiyoyori returned her gaze. She said no more, just waited calmly for him to obey her.

He said, "But you will come to me later? We will be together?"

"I promise we will," she said.

6

SHIKANOKO

After the lord left, Sesshin looked from the dead bird to Lady Tora and then to Shikanoko.

"I don't understand why you are here. I usually conduct my divinations in private. They involve secrets that only the initiated are permitted to see."

"We have something that will save you some time," Lady Tora said. "Shikanoko is an initiate. And I have taken part in rituals far more esoteric and dangerous than anything you can imagine, even though you are a great scholar and magician. Shikanoko, give the master the mask."

He handed it over, suddenly reluctant to expose Shisoku's creation to the scrutiny of another sorcerer, but Sesshin took it from the bag with reverent hands and studied it intently. "What a wonderful thing! Who made it?"

Lady Tora said, "The mountain sorcerer Shisoku. It was made for Shikanoko because he is the son of the stag."

Sesshin looked swiftly at Shikanoko as if seeing him for the first time. There was a flash of something—surprise, recognition. The old man shook his head.

"Well, well," he said quietly. "Let him put it on."

Shika recalled Shisoku's instructions and allowed the movements of the deer dance to flow through him. The others watched intently. He could still see them in the room. He was aware of his own figure, wearing the mask, looking through its eyes. The room took on the dappled light and the rich leafy smell of the forest. And then he was the stag stepping lightly between the trees, ears pricked, nostrils flared. Hawks flew overhead, shrieking loudly. The stag bounded after them. Each bound covered miles.

Shika saw the hawks fly over a great city and under the eaves of a temple set in a deep grove, beside a lake, not far from the riverbank. He read its name board: RYUSONJI. He stood on the veranda and saw, through the open doors, the hawks alight on the shoulders of a man dressed in brocade and silk robes, embroidered with dragons. They opened their beaks and sang to him in human voices.

The man peered into the brightness and said, "I am the Prince Abbot of Ryusonji, the Dragon Temple. But who are you?"

Then Sesshin was shaking him and he was once again in the old man's dusty room.

"Don't speak! Don't say who you are!"

"I wasn't going to." Shika removed the mask, held it to his brow, and thanked it before returning it to the seven-layered bag.

"I saw your lips move. You were about to speak. Never mind; who was there?"

"The Prince Abbot of Ryusonji," Shika said. "The hawk was a messenger from him. The hawks speak to him in human voices."

Sesshin breathed out slowly. "Why would the Prince Abbot be turning his attention to Kuromori?"

"Perhaps he is looking for you," Lady Tora suggested.

"I sincerely hope he doesn't know who or where I am."

"Don't be so modest, Master. Surely at one time you knew each other quite well?"

"Years ago we studied together. He will have forgotten me by now."

"Something must have reminded him. Unless it is the Kuromori lord who has attracted his attention."

Sesshin scratched his head with both hands. "I just want a quiet life," he complained. "I don't want to come to the attention of the Prince Abbot. He's going to be very angry at the loss of his werehawk. It is dead, isn't it?" He poked at the bird, but it gave no sign of life. "You shouldn't have killed it."

"Only Shikanoko could have killed it, and he was there," Lady Tora said. "Doesn't that suggest some deeper working of fate than your desire for a quiet life?"

Sesshin buried his head in his hands. "I would like you to go away now while I consider what this means and how I should advise Lord Kiyoyori. I have a horrible feeling it is not going to turn out well, least of all for me."

"Shikanoko can leave now, but I will stay. There is

something else that needs to be done before I go to Lord Kiyoyori."

Shika wanted to stay with them, wanted to talk about what had happened to him, what it all meant, who was the priest who had seemed so alarming and so attractive at the same time. He sensed they knew so much they could teach him and he was seized by a ferocious hunger to swallow up all this knowledge before it was too late.

"Go," Lady Tora said, but he lingered outside, aware of the fragrance emanating from her, mingling with the lamp oil and incense. He heard the old man say, as if with foreboding, "What do you want from me?"

"That which you have not given to earth, water, air, or fire, to neither man nor woman, for forty years," she replied. "I am going to make you a father."

"You'll have no luck with me," he said, trying to joke. "It's all withered away."

"You will be able to give me what I need. Don't look so apprehensive, my dear Master. I promise you will find it enjoyable."

Shika walked away. He did not know if he was feeling jealousy or some other deep emotion. He felt a sob rise in his chest—was it grief? But why would he weep for Akuzenji or for any of the others who had teased and bullied him? Yet he was close to tears for them, and felt he should make some effort to honor their deaths and placate their restless spirits. He could hear chanting in the distance. Following the sound, he made his way to the small shrine at the end of the lake, and knelt there beneath the cedars.

7

KIYOYORI

The last of the bodies were stacked in a pile, covered with brushwood, and set on fire. It had been a long time since the smell of burning flesh floated over the peaceful dwellings and fields of Matsutani. Kiyoyori was impatient, racked by desire, but he would not let this distract him from what had to be done. He dispatched groups of retainers with the heads to display them on sharpened posts at the Shimaura barrier and at crossroads and bridges along the North Mountain Road. Then he turned his attention to the problems that the deaths of Akuzenji and his band presented. The most urgent matter was to launch an attack on their mountain fortress and secure for himself their means of controlling the road and the merchants who traveled along it. This seemed like a straightforward exercise that could be carried out by his retainers. Then arrangements had to be made to purify the riding ground from the pollution of death and to make offerings to placate the spirits of the departed. When he had issued his instructions and spoken to the priests, he sent for his wife. By then it was approaching dusk.

"Your eyes are red," he addressed her. "Were you weeping because I was not killed?"

"Forgive me, lord. I was overcome by shock and grief that such an attempt should be made on my husband's life."

"And you are no doubt affected by the death of one of your waiting-women?"

"If she was in any way part of the intrigue I rejoice at her death. My tears are for no one but you."

"I would like to believe that."

"It is true." An expression of fear flickered into her eyes as though she had suddenly realized the danger of her position.

"You did not for a moment allow yourself to hope that you might be returned to your first husband?"

"How can you say such a thing? He is as dead to me. Have I not been a faithful wife to you? Everything that was mine is now yours. I have given you a son; I have been a mother to your daughter, as far as she would let me. I would have gladly given you more children, but you seem to have grown cold toward me."

He made no reply, studying her carefully. She met his gaze with frank eyes.

"My lord must be tired and hungry. Let me prepare a bath and some food. What is your pleasure?"

"Did you know that my brother had been sending letters to Enryo?"

"I swear I did not. I would have told you at once. Please, take a bath and relax. Shall I bring the children to see you?"

The cedar-scented smoke from the bathhouse masked the smell from the pyre, and in the hot water Kiyoyori felt himself cleansed in body and spirit. He ate with his children, who were thrilled and grateful to be included in the special feast his wife prepared: rice with chestnuts and quail, hen's eggs simmered in broth, freshwater fish grilled with taro. They were well behaved and confident. Both seemed intelligent, especially Hina, who he could see was growing more like her mother every day. She showed a great interest in the events of the day and questioned him closely about what they all meant, what would happen to the boy who shot the bird, and what her father would do with all the extra horses.

He could find no fault in their upbringing. But how would he feel if their mother was betraying him? He recalled Sesshin's words. *Your brother will be back in Matsutani and your children will be dead.*

This had become the usual behavior of warlords and warriors. Was it not how he had dealt with Akuzenji? Even now his men were clearing out the mountain fortress as though ridding it of vermin. If Akuzenji had children there none would remain alive. He felt a moment of futile regret, which he tried to put from him. He could not show any weakness, or he would be exploited by those he spared or by the others among whom he strove to be first, most important, most powerful. He would reap the benefit of his victory today and bestow the land and resources he gained as a reward to one or other of his men to bind them closer to him. He wondered as he did from time to time what his life would have been like if his father had agreed to his request to become a monk. He might have known greater peace and fewer regrets, he would have no suspicions of his wife or rage against those who sought to betray him, but he would not taste the incomparable elation of success or the restless anticipation of his next encounter with the new woman.

After they had finished eating, his wife told the maids to prepare the bedding and take the children away. When they were alone she encouraged Kiyoyori to lie down, and he saw that she wanted to lie alongside him and make love to him. But she was not the one he desired, and he felt ashamed of sleeping while his men were still out risking their lives.

"I think I will go to the shrine for a while," he said. "I cannot come close to you when death and blood lie so heavy on me."

"Whatever Lord Kiyoyori wishes," she said, trying to hide her disappointment, but failing.

※

The priests were chanting, incense burned, and bells rang. Kiyoyori noticed a solitary figure kneeling at some distance from the shrine steps beneath the tall, shadowy cedar trees. He washed his hands and rinsed his mouth at the cistern. An attendant rushed forward with a mat for him to kneel on. After he had prayed for his victims' souls he asked to have Shikanoko sent to him.

He spoke some words to comfort him. "I made arrangements for prayers to be offered. May their souls have a safe onward journey."

"I cannot believe they are all dead," the boy said in a low voice. "They are all dead and I am alive. Though perhaps it is your intention to send me to join them."

"Tell me who you are and how you came to be with them, and then I will decide what to do with you."

Shikanoko told him his story briefly, and when he had finished Kiyoyori said, "That is rather inconvenient, as your uncle is one of my chief allies. He swore allegiance to me and I confirmed him in the estate after you were presumed dead."

"But Kumayama is mine," Shikanoko replied.

"Nevertheless your uncle, Jiro no Sademasa, has been loyal to me. I cannot simply evict him in your favor."

"Even though he tried to kill me?" Shikanoko said stubbornly.

"We have only your word for that. Your uncle's version is you slipped and fell. In his opinion it was a result of your willful and impetuous character, and was an accident that would have happened sooner or later. Furthermore, why should I or anyone else believe you? You could be an imposter, put up to this claim by your bandit master. What proof do you have that you are Kazumaru?"

"People will recognize me. My men will know me."

"Your men are quite happy with your uncle. Boys change in the year between sixteen and seventeen. The boy who disappeared was a child. I see before me a man with all the appearance of an outlaw."

"So, you do intend to kill me?"

"I have not yet decided."

The boy said nothing. He did not plead or argue and Kiyoyori liked him for that. He was disposed to spare him—good bowmen were always useful, and Shikanoko had possibly done him a favor by shooting down the werehawk.

"Was anything revealed in the divination?" he asked.

"They sent me away after the mask showed us the bird's identity. There was another ritual to perform between Lady Tora and the master."

Lady Tora. So that was her name.

"What kind of ritual?" Kiyoyori said.

Shikanoko did not answer for a moment but shot a strange look at the lord as though their roles were reversed and Kiyoyori were the youth whose life hung in the balance.

"And just who is the so-called lady?" Kiyoyori asked. *A bandit's woman*, he was thinking. *Mine by right of conquest.*

"Lord Kiyoyori should be wary. Lady Tora is not what she seems."

Night was falling and it had grown much colder. The wind had swung around to the north and dark rain clouds were slowly covering the sky. A sudden gust sent dead leaves swirling beneath the trees.

Kiyoyori stood. "Let us go and learn the results of the divination."

He was seized by impatience and alarm that the "ritual" might be a euphemism for something unbearable—and so it was. When he strode into the room and saw the woman and Sesshin lying in disarray and realized what they had been doing, his rage was so great, he felt like killing them both. But Lady Tora smiled and said, "And now, lord, I am yours," and prostrated herself before him as she had done before. The same lust erupted within him. He grabbed her hand and led her through the garden, where she seemed to fly behind him, so light was her hold on his. He took her to a building on the lakeshore, the summer pavilion.

Rain drove against the shutters. Drops fell through the flimsy roof, making the charcoal in the brazier smoke and hiss. Beneath the bearskin rugs Kiyoyori and Tora were remote in their own world. He had not lain with a woman for months; his wife no longer attracted him and he had been too preoccupied to seek pleasure elsewhere. Now he was possessed by the mindless lust of adolescence, the inexhaustible desire, yet it was more than lust; it was a passionate yearning to be completely absorbed by this woman, to surrender to her and let her take him to unimaginable destinations.

He had thought her the bandit's woman, a prostitute, and when he had walked into the scholar's room and saw that Sesshin, the old fox, had been making love to her, he had been angry but also strangely relieved. So she was a whore; he desired her, he would take her, and when he was tired of her, he would have her executed along with the boy. But when the night was beginning to fade into dawn and his desire was finally sated, she stroked his hair and sang quietly, one of the songs that were popular in the capital, and he felt he had found the other half of himself, that he would tire of his own body before he tired of her. He lay making plans for the future; he would build her a house and install her there as his second wife.

He foolishly did not consider that she might have her own plans.

8

AKIHIME

The eldest daughter of the Nishimi family was tradition-
ally dedicated to the shrine of the All-Merciful Kannon
at Rinrakuji to become a shrine maiden. The family was
among the highest rank of the nobility, related to the Emperor. The current head of the household, Hidetake, was a
close friend of the Crown Prince, Momozono, and his wife
was wet nurse to the Crown Prince's son, Yoshimori.

Hidetake had had two daughters born some ten years
apart. The older one was called Akihime, the Autumn
Princess, because she had been born in the autumn, the
same month as now, when the maples were turning scarlet
and the ginkgo tree by the gate dropped swathes of golden
leaves. The younger one, born in winter, had died at birth.
It was because of this that her mother had been able to
nurse the young prince, the Emperor's grandson.

Aki was fifteen years old, not particularly beautiful

but lively and full of high spirits. In that autumn of her sixteenth year, suitors had begun to hover outside the house, wooing with poetry and music. Her mother both feared and hoped that one might find his way in. It was the custom of that time: if a man came three nights in a row and made love to the girl, it was considered a marriage. Aki had already made her vows of purity and she recoiled from the idea yet was drawn to it at the same time. Were the men invited inside or did they force their way in? Did the girl have any choice in the matter or did she simply submit?

"I won't let anyone touch me," she declared one morning when her mother was voicing her concerns. "You know my father has taught me how to defend myself."

"You can hardly fight off a young nobleman with a sword," her mother exclaimed. "That would be a terrible scandal." Then she added with a sigh, "Sometimes we don't want to defend ourselves. Men can be very persistent. But at least if that happened we could keep you at home."

Aki could see her mother was close to tears. "You will still have Yoshimori, and Kai, who is like a daughter to you."

They both looked over to the veranda, where Kai was playing with Yoshimori. They had been born on the same day and were inseparable friends. Yoshimori was in his seventh year. He was an intelligent child, popular with everyone, adored by his father. When he was two years old a physiognomist had pronounced that he would reign as emperor. It had made a deep impression on him.

"Yoshimori will soon be lost to me," her mother said.

"But I suppose I will never lose Kai, as no one will ever marry her."

"You can't see her ears when her hair covers them. I think they are charming, like a little bird or a gecko."

"A gecko! Don't say such things!"

Kai's mother, one of the women of the household of whom Aki's mother had been particularly fond, had died in childbirth. Her baby girl had tiny ears like the whorl of a shell. When the midwives saw her they had exclaimed in fear, and the baby had been wrapped in a cloth and left in a corner. It had been a terrible day, with the deaths of a mother and a child and the birth, earlier than expected, of the young prince. Kai's mother was buried the same day as Aki's little sister, while the baby prince was given to Aki's mother to nurse. Everyone forgot the other baby, but she clung to life until Aki's mother heard her whimpers and demanded to see her. She was moved to pity and insisted that she would bring up both children together.

They were afraid she might be deaf, but she could hear perfectly well though she had a way of frowning and looking intently at people's mouths when they spoke to her. She was prettier than Aki, with a sweet, plump face and delicate limbs, and the women of the household often bewailed the fact that she might have made a wonderful marriage or other alliance, maybe even with Yoshimori himself, but for her ears.

No one knew what the future would bring for her, but Yoshimori adored her, insisted that she be with him at all times, and often would be calmed and consoled by only her. She had a lively imagination and made up stories and games, keeping him entertained in what was otherwise a tedious existence for a young child. He was not allowed outside—the veranda was as far as he went—and he was carried everywhere within the palace. He saw his own parents rarely and then had to be carefully trained in the correct etiquette and elaborate language of the court. Already he was expected to take part in the long, complicated rituals that were part of life in the Imperial Household and, though he was not yet seven years old, sometimes Aki saw on his face an expression of resignation and world-weariness that moved her to pity. Only with Kai did he behave like an ordinary child. He ordered her around, squabbled with her, threatened to scream if he was separated from her, but they ate from the same bowl and slept side by side.

Aki knew his father, Crown Prince Momozono, a little, though she was not allowed to speak of how. Her father had taken her to Rinrakuji several times. She had made her preliminary vows there and begun to learn her duties and the many rituals in the service of Kannon. She was taught self-defense, how to ride a horse, and how to use a bow. Her father practiced sword fighting and studied the art of war with an old monk who had once been a famous warrior. Sometimes Prince Momozono was there, too, in disguise. Rinrakuji's monks had the reputation of being bold and belligerent, and Aki knew without being told that her father and the Prince were preparing for war.

The Emperor, Momozono's father, was ailing. He had

designated his oldest son as his heir, but the Prince Abbot, the powerful priest at the temple of Ryusonji, favored the second son, Daigen, whose mother was the Prince Abbot's sister. He had formed an implacable dislike to the Crown Prince, taking every opportunity to undermine him, trying to persuade the Emperor to disinherit him. Aki knew that Prince Momozono was preparing to fight for the throne if necessary, but that no one must reveal this, for if it came to the Prince Abbot's ears it would be called rebellion.

"Look!" Yoshi called, pointing into the garden. "Look at that strange bird."

Aki stared out and saw a large black bird that had landed clumsily in one of the maple trees, scattering leaves and twigs. It gave a curious call, both compelling and repulsive, and swung its head toward Yoshimori as if studying his features with its hard golden eyes. It seemed to recognize him, for it bowed its head three times in a way that was both respectful and mocking.

Aki's mother and her attendants were seized by horror, for it seemed a terrible omen, but Kai, unafraid, cried, "Let's give it something to eat."

"Yes, bring food!" Yoshimori commanded.

One of the ladies-in-waiting went inside, pale-faced and trembling, and came back with a bowl of rice cakes. Kai took one and went slowly into the garden. Yoshimori tried to follow her, but at least three pairs of hands restrained him.

Kai held the rice cake on her open palm. The bird peered down. When it did not descend she placed the cake on the ground and took a few steps back. The bird hopped from the tree, picked up the rice cake in its claws, inspected it carefully, then swallowed it in a gulp. It fluttered to the pond and drank. Then it flew back to the maple, preened its breast feathers, and continued to watch balefully, occasionally uttering a loud shriek.

"I don't like it," Yoshi said. "Make it go away."

The women clapped their hands and raised their voices, but the bird would not be dislodged.

"Go call your father," Aki's mother said. "It's giving me a headache. And what terrible disasters does it portend?"

Aki found her father and told him the news, then asked, "Should I bring my bow?" It was the ceremonial catalpa bow she had been given at the temple, along with a ritual box that held a doll, a weasel's skull, and her prayer beads.

"Yes, and I'll bring mine," her father replied, but when he saw the bird he laid the bow aside quickly, even furtively. He stepped out into the garden and said angrily, "How dare you come here? Go tell your master to cease trying to spy on me!"

Aki raised her bow and twanged the string as she had been taught, to alert the spirits. The bird swung its head toward her, gave a scornful cry, and flew away to the north.

"What was it, Father?" Aki said, going to stand at his side, following his gaze as the bird disappeared.

"A werehawk, a sort of magic hawk. The Prince Abbot has several at his command. They have speech of a sort that only he can understand. Vile birds! I hate them!"

"You should have shot it, Father."

"I did not want to show I am armed and prepared to use my bow. They are almost impossible to kill anyway." He said in a quieter voice, "He is suspicious of me. What will he do next? I am glad you will soon be at Rinrakuji. You will be out of his reach, and what you learn there may help us in our struggle against him."

Aki shivered as if she sensed a dark shadow stretching out over the city from Ryusonji.

9

TAMA

Like most girls of that time who lived in the provinces, Tama had been taught to ride and fight with a lance. When she came of age, her mother had presented her with a dagger so she could defend herself or take her own life if necessary. The only time she had been tempted to use it was when she and the estate she had inherited had been taken from her husband and given to his older brother. She had lain awake at night, furious in her helplessness, imagining plunging the dagger into the throat that lay exposed next to her. She had never contemplated killing herself, for to do so would be to lose Matsutani, the family home where she had grown up and which she loved passionately.

She waited for love to develop for Kiyoyori. She could see rationally that he was an admirable man. He was courageous and intelligent, kind to his daughter, good-looking in a way, though not as handsome as his younger brother. But love never came; it had come once, for Masachika, and her heart refused to be unfaithful though her body had to be. Even after their son, Tsumaru, was born, she felt only indifference for her husband. Now she was also afraid of him. Since the attack by Akuzenji and the apparent disloyalty of Enryo and his wife, his suspicions of her had increased. She had to conceal her grief for her friend and her anger at her husband. She was determined that she would give him no excuse to kill her.

She knew she did not love Tsumaru passionately as some mothers seemed to, and Hina was always cool toward her, but she made sure the children were brought up properly. She prided herself on carrying out her duties. She oversaw the running of the household, the making of clothes, the supplies of food and charcoal, the pleasure gardens, rice paddies, and vegetable fields. She made the most of the life that had been given to her, tried to shut away all memories of Masachika, and was not unhappy, until the arrival of the sorceress who had enthralled Kiyoyori with a single look and who now lived in the summer pavilion.

Tama hated this woman for her supernatural beauty and strangeness, for her self-confidence, her indifference to everyone but Kiyoyori, for the way she had taken up residence as spiders and foxes move into deserted houses. Sometimes Tama took out the dagger and felt its sharp edge, and imagined slashing that beautiful face to ribbons. She imagined setting fire to the pavilion, and ordered the winter's firewood to be stored along its southwestern side. Her loathing embraced the old scholar. Until now she had paid little attention to him though his presence in her well-ordered home irritated her. He had come without permission or invitation; he upset the maids by never allowing them to clean his room, and she disliked his sharp eyes and his air of superiority. Now she suspected him of some close connection with Kiyoyori's woman. She sensed that they were two of a kind, both involved in sorcery. Her dislike included Shikanoko, even though Hina and Tsumaru admired him and followed him around while he cared for the horses and carried out Lady Tora's orders. He seemed to tolerate their company and was patient with them, but Tama still disapproved and tried to forbid it. The children, however, were adept at disappearing outside, and Hina, she was sure, took pleasure in disobeying her.

She began to watch Shikanoko obsessively, following him as much as the children did, resenting how assiduously he served Lady Tora. She saw how, after Kiyoyori had decided he should live, Shikanoko had been given the choice of Akuzenji's horses and had taken the white stallion for himself, as well as the brown mare. She thought the horses gave him undeserved status, the right to be fed along with the rest of Kiyoyori's men; she knew he slept on the veranda outside the summer pavilion while her husband was within, and that he was aware of her as she prowled jealously through the gardens.

In the tenth month Kiyoyori decided to go to Miyako. It would probably be the last chance he would have before the snow came, and he had said he was disturbed by rumors of intrigue and unrest, which he wanted to investigate for himself. Hina moped and had bad dreams. A few days after his departure the weather was suddenly fine and warm and, feeling it was the last of the pleasant autumn days, Tama allowed the children to play outside. They did not return for the midday meal, but she assumed they were eating with their former nurse, Haru. Haru had two children of the same age, Chika and Kaze, and the four often played together. She was busy overseeing the fulling of cloth, and reflecting, as the heavy sound rang out in the still air, how peaceful Matsutani was, when one of the maids approached her.

"Lady, the children are not back yet."

"Where is Shikanoko? They are probably trailing after him somewhere."

"The men say he went out earlier with his horses," the girl replied. "He didn't take the children."

"They must be at Haru's. Go and get them; it will be dark soon and it is time they came home."

"Lady," the girl said nervously. "I have been to Haru. They are not there. They called at her door in the morning, but her two children are sick, so she told them not to come in. She thinks they might have gone up toward the Darkwood. Her husband is out looking for them."

The first sense of unease pricked her and immediately she began assigning blame. Kiyoyori should not have left them so unprotected; he should never have let that woman into their home, or, come to that, the old man Sesshin. Some sorcery was at work. Shikanoko had stolen them. They had been abducted by foxes or wild mountain men for secret rituals, to be carved up or eaten. She began to run toward Haru's house. From the forest she could hear men's voices calling hauntingly. *Tsumaru! Oh-e! Hina!* But the only response was the whir of a startled pheasant and the hooting of owls as dusk fell.

Then from the other direction, from the road that led west, she heard shouts that were more relieved, joyful in tone.

They have been found!

She ran back to the west gate and saw a cluster of people hurrying toward her, carrying . . . *O Merciful Heaven, not a corpse! And only one? Where is the other?*

It was Hina; she looked limp, lifeless, and Tama feared the worst. Her heart was threatening to choke her, but the child stirred when she took her in her arms. She was alive. She had been struck on the temple, the bruise already darkening the pale, delicate skin. She opened her eyes and stared vacantly at her stepmother. Her pupils were dilated and she did not seem to know where she was.

"Hina," Tama cried. "What happened? Where is Tsumaru?"

Light came back into the child's stare. "Mother," she said haltingly. "Men took him. I tried to stop them. One of them smacked me."

"What sort of men? What did they look like? Was Shikanoko with them?"

"No! He would have protected us. It wasn't him. Oh, my head hurts so much!"

Kongyo, Haru's husband, arrived at Tama's side. "Lady, I would it had been my son."

"Why was no one watching them?" she said in anger. "How can one child be snatched away and the other left for dead, and no one saw?"

"They often hide," Kongyo said. "It's no excuse, I know, but it's a game they play. They can cross the whole estate without anyone seeing them."

"Your children taught them this! They must be punished!"

"Whatever my lady commands."

"Ride to the capital," she cried, with a mixture of dread and anger. "Lord Kiyoyori must be told."

"It is almost dark, Lady Tama."

"Take torches! Ride all night! And remember, your children are now hostages to me."

She herself carried Hina inside and then gave her to her waiting-women, who laid her carefully down and began to apply compresses soaked in vinegar to the bruise. The girl vomited once or twice, pale, pearl-hued strands unlike any food she might have eaten, and then fell into a deep sleep.

Tama stared obsessively at the black eyelashes quivering against the fragile skin, through which she could see the faint blue veins where the blood pulsed slowly, and listened to the unnaturally heavy breathing. She shook Hina gently, but the girl did not waken. Slowly the conviction grew within Tama that her stepdaughter had been placed under a spell.

"Where is Shikanoko?" she cried. When she was told he had not returned, she commanded, "Bring the old man to me."

10

SHIKANOKO

Shikanoko had taken the horses out in the late afternoon, as he often did, training Nyorin to know his voice and respond to his commands. He had just got back and was feeding them, planning to go next to Lady Tora to see if she had any requests for him before night fell, when he saw Sesshin, already in his night attire, being escorted to Lady Tama's rooms. A tense atmosphere had descended over Matsutani. Grooms were preparing horses and blazing torches. He saw Kongyo ride off at a gallop with three other men. Nyorin whinnied loudly, watching their departure with raised head and nervous eyes.

Tora stepped out of the summer pavilion onto the narrow veranda. Shikanoko saw the curve of her belly against the western light.

"What's happened?" he said.

"Lady Tama's son has disappeared. I suppose someone has taken him to persuade his father to submit to his will."

He glanced up at her face, disconcerted by the indifference in her voice.

She smoothed the robe over her belly. "I will give him more sons," she said. "You had better follow Master Sesshin and make sure he comes to no harm."

Shikanoko went to the residence. In the confusion no one had thought to close the shutters, and from where he stood outside he could clearly see and hear everything that was happening within.

He heard Tama's voice. "You are so wise, Master Sesshin, and my husband admires you so much. Why have you repaid him in this vile way?"

"Lady," the old man replied, "this has nothing to do with me. If I can be blamed for anything it is my failure to put adequate protection around Lord Kiyoyori's children, which I regret deeply."

"That is crime enough—you admit you could have protected them and did not?"

"Even I cannot foresee all the evil deeds of men," Sesshin said. "Don't be too anxious. The boy must have been taken for a purpose. Therefore he is in no immediate danger."

"How do you know this? You are involved! Shikanoko took them, didn't he?"

"I am simply making deductions. Neither Shikanoko nor I had anything to do with it."

Tama stared at him for a moment and then said abruptly, "Release Hina from the spell she is under."

"Let me look at her," the old man said, and then, "She

is concussed. It is not a spell. She will wake in the morning, fully recovered. Your women have done the right thing—vinegar compresses, nothing better. I believe you have sent for Lord Kiyoyori. There is nothing else that can be done now. We should all get some sleep. Forgive me, as I grow older my eyes grow weary."

Shika heard something snap in the lady's voice as she replied. "Weary? Oh, let me cure you of that. Let me show you how it feels to lose the light of your eyes, that which is dearest to you."

She turned to the men who had brought Sesshin to her. "Put them out."

They did not understand. "Lady?" one queried.

"Put out his eyes." She drew out her dagger and held it to her throat. "Do as I say or I will take my own life. Explain that to Lord Kiyoyori when he returns."

Shika wanted to call out: *Don't obey her! Let her kill herself. You will be doing the lord a favor.* But they were retainers from her household, accustomed to following her commands without question, and besides, he thought, seeing their faces, there was not one among them who shrank from the idea of blinding a man accused of sorcery.

He heard one sharp cry of agony, then another. He could not prevent himself from running forward. The men pushed Sesshin, his face streaming blood, off the veranda and threw the useless globes after him. Lady Tama came forward to watch the old man scrabble in the dirt. When she saw Shikanoko approach him she called out, "You, take him away! Let me never see either of you again!"

"My books, my books! I will never read again!" Sesshin's chest was heaving as he moaned.

Shika knelt beside him, his heart expanding and contracting with such force he felt it would burst from his chest. He was engulfed by pity and horror. "I will get some for you. I will read to you. Tell me what I should bring." His reassurances sounded futile and hollow in his own ears. He said dully, "It is I, Shikanoko."

"You will take nothing," Tama commanded. "I will burn it all. Now go before I add you to the fire!"

Sesshin reached out, feeling for him, and grabbed his arm. "Shikanoko," he whispered. "Pick up my eyes and bring them. And fetch a blanket or a jacket, the night will be cold."

Shika gathered up the eyes, his heart twisting in pity. No one came near him or offered any help. Indeed, they stood back and turned their faces away. Only a servant girl, who had often attended to the old man, brought a bowl of warm water and some clean cloths. Shika bathed Sesshin's face and tore a strip to make a bandage. He could feel him trembling from shock and pain. Then he washed the eyes, while tears streamed from his own and the girl wept.

"Fasten them to the west gate," Sesshin said, "so they may continue to watch over this place when we are gone."

Shika had been ordered to take Sesshin away, but now he was worried about Lady Tora. Lord Kiyoyori had commanded him to look after her. Leaving Sesshin for a few minutes with the girl, despite her protests, he ran to the summer pavilion.

He was able to release the horses but could not get any

closer; it was surrounded by guards and some were already putting torches to the pile of firewood.

"Where is Lady Tora?" he said to one of them.

"Inside, we hope."

"Lord Kiyoyori will have your heads for this," he said in fury.

"And I'll have yours, you bandit scum, if you don't get out of here."

Windows and doors were all firmly fastened. There was no sign of movement within.

She will have escaped, he thought. *She would not let them trap her, especially not if she bears the lord's child. But where is she?*

He could stay and fight for her—if she was there—or he could escape with Sesshin. He made the decision, instantly regretting it, but not wavering. He hastened to collect his few possessions, sword and bow, the bag containing the mask, and saddled the horses. The servant girl met him halfway back.

"Hurry," she said. "They are talking of killing you."

He lifted Sesshin onto Risu's back, tied him so he would not fall, and led both horses to the west gate. Risu was fretful; she did not want to go out in the dark, but the big stallion remained calm, and where he went she followed.

There were many people milling around, carrying armfuls of books, boxes and flasks, maps and charts that he recognized from Sesshin's rooms. They were taking them to the summer pavilion and adding them to the firewood, already ablaze. No one looked at them as they passed under the gate.

Its transept was carved below the roof with curling

dragons and flowers. Shika stood on Nyorin's back and found a niche into which he could slip the two eyes.

Sesshin had not uttered a word, but now he said, "Make sure you behave yourselves. I am leaving my eyes to watch you, so don't think you can get away with anything."

"Who are you talking to?"

"I put some guardian spirits in the gates when I came to Matsutani. Migi and Hidari are their names. They're quite effective, but they need a lot of supervision."

Shika was shivering when he sat down again and took up the lead rope. It was almost completely dark.

"Where shall we go?" he wondered aloud. As soon as it was light he could find food, but they would need water. It was too dark to ride all night—it was the time of the new moon. He thought of the woodland pools he knew where deer and other animals would come to drink at dawn, and decided he would follow the stream that flowed into the lake from the northeast and find one of its pools in the Darkwood.

They circled around the back of the residence, following the wall, their way lit by the flames as the summer pavilion burned.

When they entered the Darkwood, Sesshin said, "We have been delivered from the Prince Abbot in a truly miraculous way."

"Miraculous? You have lost your sight and all your possessions. Lady Tora has vanished and we are fugitives!"

"But now we know the true nature of existence," Sesshin said. "And that is an inestimable gift."

11

KIYOYORI

When he arrived in the capital, Kiyoyori went first to the palace of the Kakizuki, to pay his respects to the head of his family, Lord Keita. He bowed to the great lord from some distance and received a gracious acknowledgment, and was then summoned to the apartment of one of his senior counselors, Hosokawa no Masafusa, who was some kind of cousin to Kiyoyori's father.

Like all the Kakizuki, Masafusa lived in great luxury, wore robes of brocade and damask of the kind that were once reserved for members of the imperial family, served elegant food on gold and celadon dishes, and provided an endless supply of wine, music, and entertainers.

Masafusa told him all the usual gossip in his barbed, amusing way, but Kiyoyori felt he had something more pressing, and at the end of the meal his suspicions were proved true.

Masafusa lowered his voice and said, "Your brother has submitted a claim to the estate of Matsutani to the tribunal in Minatogura."

"What tribunal?" Kiyoyori replied.

"It was set up by the Miboshi to deal with land disputes in an organized and legal way. You must know Miboshi Aritomo has a passion for legality and administration."

"He can have all the passion he likes, that doesn't give him and his tribunal jurisdiction over Matsutani."

"I don't think there's any cause for alarm, but you needed to be informed."

"Even if the tribunal finds in favor of my brother, which I find hard to believe, he would have to resort to arms to get possession. I am perfectly capable of defending both my estates, Matsutani and Kuromori. And I imagine I could expect help from the capital. After all, Matsutani stands between Miyako and Minatogura. If it fell to Miboshi allies, it would leave Miyako wide open to attack."

Masafusa nodded. "Of course, we are aware of all this."

Kiyoyori mused for a few moments, then said, "Why is the claim being heard now? Are the Miboshi so confident of being able to distribute land currently under Kakizuki control? Are they planning something?"

"The Emperor is not well," Masafusa whispered. "There is going to be a challenge over the succession."

"But the Crown Prince is the most suitable, as well as the rightful heir."

"Indeed. We have not seen a future emperor of such talent and intelligence for many years. And his wife is Kaki-

zuki, Lord Keita's eldest daughter. But certain persons—
I do not want to name any names—favor his younger
brother."

Certain persons who dwell in Ryusonji, Kiyoyori thought.

"We are facing war," he said, a statement rather than a
question.

"You should be prepared for anything," Masafusa replied. "Our lord is aware of your loyalty and devotion." He
did not, however, make any commitments or offers of support in the way of armed warriors and horses.

Kiyoyori returned to the house he kept in the city, below Rokujo, angered and disturbed by this conversation.
The Miboshi were preparing to challenge the Kakizuki
in the capital itself. They were so confident of success, they
were already redistributing land in their law courts. And
their most powerful ally, the Prince Abbot, had already
turned his attention to Matsutani.

He felt he should return without delay to Matsutani,
but he was also needed in the capital. He was angered by
Keita and Masafusa's apparent lack of concern. Would the
Miboshi and the Prince Abbot really dare attack Prince
Momozono? And would the Kakizuki have the ability and
the will to defend him?

Even though he had sent some of his men on ahead, the
house felt unusually cold and unlived in. Servants were
often unreliable, but it was unlike his steward to let him
down. He remembered when the man, Taro, from the insignificant village of Iida, had joined his household. He had
seen something in his bold eyes and cunning expression

that appealed to him, and his trust had been justified. Taro could read and write well, had many connections in the city, and was often a source of information that Kiyoyori would not have learned from anyone else. He was about to call for him when the man appeared, sliding open the inner door and saying, "Lord Kiyoyori, a messenger is here for you from Ryusonji. The Prince Abbot has summoned you."

"Now? At this time of night? What does he want?"

"I have not been able to find out," Taro replied in a whisper, indicating the monk half-hidden in the shadows. "But someone must have seen you arrive in the city and thought it important enough to inform the Prince Abbot."

"I suppose I must go," Kiyoyori said. "But if I don't return you had better inform my wife what happened to me."

She will have Masachika restored to her, he thought with pain. *And what will become of my children? And Lady Tora?*

The idea of never seeing Tora again was unbearable, but he could hardly send messages to her through Taro. Surely she was thinking of him, as he thought constantly of her, and neither of them would die without the other knowing.

The horses walked nervously, with pricked ears and exaggerated steps, shying at shadows. It was a cold night, the new moon a thin sliver in the east. He could smell the frost in the air, turning the breath of men and horses to cloud. The stars glittered, pinpricks in the curtain of the sky.

Ryusonji was close to the river and had been founded at the place where a dragon child fell to earth. The dragon's spirit lived in a lake in the gardens. People believed only the greatest magicians could summon it up and use its power. The Prince Abbot was one of them. He was the Emperor's brother-in-law and combined in his person all the prestige of the imperial family with the wealth and influence of the sect to which Ryusonji belonged.

They left the horses at the outer gate and walked through gardens and courtyards lit by oil lamps on stands. Guards and servants waited silently on the verandas. One stepped forward and made a sign to Kiyoyori's men to stop, and he was led forward alone. He was half-expecting to be seized, interrogated, and executed, which was what normally happened to people summoned to Ryusonji in the middle of the night. He had no idea what he had done, but obviously he had somehow come to the attention of the Prince Abbot. First the werehawk had been sent, and now he himself had been brought here.

He was, however, treated courteously and shown into the reception room where the Prince Abbot sat on a small raised platform matted with fresh, sweet-smelling straw and decorated with purple and white silk cushions. On the walls hung scrolls of sacred texts and pictures of protective deities, predominantly dragons. A golden statue of the Enlightened One stood in an alcove, flanked by vases of chrysanthemums. Gilt and jewels glittered in the lamplight.

Kiyoyori bowed to the ground and waited for the priest to speak.

His voice was high-pitched but measured as he gave Kiyoyori permission to sit up, every syllable enunciated clearly, his language that of the court. His face was rather long, his complexion pale. His shaven head was covered by a priest's cap, richly embroidered like his clothes. He thanked Kiyoyori for coming, commented on the night temperature (which was plummeting—there was no heating of any sort in the room), and then fell silent, contemplating the younger man's face.

Finally he said, "Well, Lord Kiyoyori of Kuromori, tell me what you are up to in your Darkwood."

"My lord?"

"You are dabbling in matters you do not understand. I want to know who is leading you astray." His voice had not lost its calm politeness, but there was menace behind the words.

"I am not sure what Your Eminence is talking about. My estate is small and insignificant, but within it I am the master. If I go astray it is my own doing. No one leads me."

"I know differently," the Prince Abbot replied. "Let me be frank with you. I am an adept in these matters. I see what is happening in all the worlds. I have messengers that fly throughout this realm and bring information back to me. Not long ago I sent one of these to Matsutani—I had become aware of powerful forces that threatened to come together in a way that bodes disaster for our Emperor's realm. It did not return, but, around the time it should have reached your estate, a stag came into my room at night and stared me in the eye. It disappeared before it could tell me who had sent it, but I believe it was someone from your house. I prayed and meditated on these events and came to the conclusion that you have within your walls—

you probably have not even noticed: for all your boasts of independence you seem remarkably unperceptive—some being, or beings, possibly not fully human, who are practicing evil magic."

Kiyoyori could not prevent a shudder, remembering the hideous werehawk and the events that had followed its death. He realized that all he felt and thought was transparent to the priest.

I must not think of Tora.

But immediately passion swept through him and he longed for her. He knew he had failed to mask it when he saw the Prince Abbot's contemptuous smile.

"They have bought you with sexual pleasure? I would have thought the Kuromori lord's price would be higher." He leaned forward. "You are in grave danger, but you can save yourself. First, those beings must be captured and handed over to me. My men will accompany you when you go home. Then you must be reconciled to your brother. His claim to Matsutani is very strong and the Miboshi will recognize it. Your father's decision was both foolish and high-handed. No one blames you for it, but you must return the estate and the wife. I suggest you retire from the world, shave your head, and make atonement for all your father's mistakes and your own."

Kiyoyori thought, *That was my original desire, but it certainly is not now!* He said nothing, trying to judge how best to respond to this outrageous request, which he had no intention of obeying.

The Prince Abbot mistook his silence for acquiescence

and after a few moments went on. "The Kakizuki have been all-powerful in the capital for many years, but their influence is waning. Their arrogance and lack of justice have turned many against them. Warriors flood the capital seeking compensation for their services, but the Kakizuki spend all their money on their own ostentatious pleasures. The Miboshi rule by law and reward those who serve them fairly. I intend my nephew to be the next emperor, and that may be sooner than was thought, very sadly, of course. I am giving you a chance to be on the winning side. Take it for the sake of your children, if not your own."

"I am amazed that Your Eminence should concern yourself with my welfare," Kiyoyori murmured.

Somewhere not far away a child was crying. It had been crying for some time, but he had not registered the sound, partly because it had been so unexpected. Now his blood turned to ice; he thought he recognized it as his son. Disbelief and bewilderment shook him physically. He half-rose, gazing toward the interior of the temple.

"Don't be alarmed. We will not harm him if you obey me." The Prince Abbot struck a bronze bowl at his side and, when a monk appeared, commanded, "Bring the child here. Sit down, Kiyoyori!"

Tsumaru was wearing his outdoor clothes, a jacket over a robe. They must have seized him while he was playing . . . but how was it possible? How had the children been left alone? Had someone in his household been involved?

"Father," Tsumaru cried, struggling to get away from the burly monk who held him, but the man gripped him more tightly. Tears ran down the child's cheeks, but he struggled to control his sobs.

"He is a fine boy," the Prince Abbot said, gesturing for him to be brought closer. "What a slender neck! Can you imagine the ease with which a sword would sever it? In the event he lives, I will make him my acolyte and educate him."

If I concede to my brother, that will be his only future, Kiyoyori thought wildly. *If I resist and am defeated he will die before me. I must buy time. I must agree for now. When I get home I will consult with Sesshin; he will tell me what to do.*

"It is gracious of Your Eminence to interest yourself in such a worthless child," he said, the false words scalding his tongue. "If I have your word that no harm will come to him in your care I will do everything you request. I will return at once to Matsutani."

"I suggest you go tonight, before dawn," the Prince Abbot said. "I do not want your departure to give rise to unsettling rumors."

In other words, the Kakizuki are not to be alerted. They are not to suspect that the Miboshi are to be handed a road straight into the capital.

"Father, don't go!" Tsumaru wept, and then, "Hina! Where is Hina?"

The monk put him down and he ran to Kiyoyori, burying his face against his father's leg.

"May I ask, where is my daughter?" Kiyoyori said.

"I believe she is at home," the Prince Abbot replied. "She will be recovering now."

He could feel the fury building within him. He knelt before Tsumaru and held him by the shoulders, looking into his eyes. "Don't be afraid. Continue to be brave. Soon you will be home again, too."

Tsumaru took a deep breath and nodded.

Kiyoyori touched his son's hair briefly, bowed to the Prince Abbot, and followed the monk to the outer gate where Tsuneto and Sadaike were waiting anxiously. They were joined by several more monks, one of whom carried a bird cage holding two of the same werehawks.

"We are returning to Matsutani," Kiyoyori said to his men when they looked questioningly at him.

At his own residence he told Tsuneto to assemble the rest of the warriors and horses while he went inside. The burly monk who had held Tsumaru followed him, standing and watching him insolently.

Taro, the steward, was waiting inside the room. In the dim light Kiyoyori thought he saw something in his expression beyond his obvious relief.

"I am leaving at once," Kiyoyori told him. "Pack my things. I am not sure when I will return to the capital."

"Shall I prepare some food?"

"Put something together for the journey, but we have no time to eat now."

Taro bowed, glanced at the monk, and said, "Lord Kiyoyori might wish to wash or use the privy before he leaves."

"Good idea," Kiyoyori replied.

"I will bring water and a lamp."

The monk looked after him suspiciously as if he might

scale the garden wall and escape, but Kiyoyori was not followed and for a few moments he was alone in the darkness. Then Taro appeared with a lamp and a jug, set them on a shelf, and helped Kiyoyori with his robe.

He said in a voice tinier than a gnat's, "I can get your son away."

"How did you know?" Kiyoyori whispered back.

"Someone came shortly after you left, and told me. He works in the gardens, saw the child arrive, and knew it must be your son when you were called to Ryusonji. He can show me how to get into the temple. I think I can rescue him."

"They will be watching him day and night, and they will kill him if your attempt fails."

"They will kill him anyway and you, too, once you have given them what they want. Trust me."

"Your life will be forfeit to me if he dies."

"You can take it. I give it to you freely. I did years ago when you gave me the chance to serve you."

The monk's voice echoed, closer than he had thought. "Lord Kiyoyori, we must leave."

There was no time for further discussion, either to give permission or to withhold it. Taro poured the water over Kiyoyori's hands and held out a small cloth to dry them. His touch was impersonal and he did not speak again. Kiyoyori began to feel he had imagined the whole conversation. His last glimpse of Taro was the man standing on the veranda, the lamp in one hand, the other raised in a gesture of farewell. The first cocks were crowing as they rode away in the darkness.

They were halfway home when they met Kongyo. Ki-yoyori brushed aside the man's shamefaced apologies.

"I have seen my son. He is alive. We have a little time." He could not say more, for the Prince Abbot's monks rode on either side of him.

As they descended the last pass into Matsutani they saw the smoke rising in the valley. Kiyoyori urged his horse on and came at a gallop to the west gate. He did not notice the eyes in their niche, though they saw him, saw the monks that rode with him, and noticed how he checked his horse at the sight of the charred beams and the soot-blackened edge of the lake.

His wife came out onto the main veranda, Hina beside her. The child was pale and there were still signs of the bruise on the side of her face. Kiyoyori leaped from his horse and knelt before his daughter, tenderly touched her cheek, and gazed into her eyes.

"I am sorry, Father," she said. "They took Tsumaru and I couldn't stop them."

"Tsumaru is safe," he said. "He is in the capital at Ryu-sonji." For the moment he must act as though it were true, at least until he could get rid of the monks, at least until he heard from Iida no Taro. "You were brave and I am proud of you."

He rose and looked at his wife, aware that if he spoke he would unleash a torrent of rage and grief. She met his eyes, and he saw a glint of some emotion in them, triumph, regret, remorse, a mixture of all three.

He mastered his own feelings and said, "What have you done?"

"You will thank me. I have cleaned out the nest of sorcery that had infested my—our—home."

"I may thank you, but the Prince Abbot of Ryusonji certainly will not. He sent these monks to take the scholar and the lady back to the capital in exchange for our son's life."

She took a small step back, glancing at the monk and then back at him. He saw her sudden dismay as she realized the meaning of his words.

He turned to the monk whose name he had learned was Gessho. "Those you seek are not here."

"Where are they?" Gessho demanded.

"The boy took the old man toward Kuromori," Tama said. "The woman, we believe, died in the fire."

"Once they are in the Darkwood they are beyond anyone's reach. As for the woman, show us her bones," Kiyoyori said, his voice steady. Surely Tora was not dead. He would know if she were.

"There was no trace; the fire was too fierce." Tama's chin was raised, her eyes bright with defiance.

She is not dead, he thought.

The short winter daylight was already beginning to fade. When Kiyoyori did not reply, Tama said, "You must all be weary and it is getting cold. Come inside and I will prepare food."

"We must search the house and grounds before it gets dark," Gessho said obstinately.

Kiyoyori fought down the urge to execute the monks on the spot, send their heads back to Ryusonji, and accept the consequences—Tsumaru's death, unless Taro had been successful, and an assault on his estates from both east and west. Grief threatened to overwhelm him—but surely she had escaped; surely he would see her again. He longed for her, he needed her.

There was no trace of either her or Sesshin. His wife had done her work well. The old man's room had been cleared out, the books, potions, flasks, bones, powders, and everything else had been burned. Gessho made no effort to hide his annoyance. However, in his search he finally came upon the eyes.

He called Kiyoyori and they both stared at the globes, which still shone, and moved and saw. While the monks, not daring to touch them, said prayers and chanted sutras, Kiyoyori went straight to Tama's rooms.

"What else did you do?" he said. "Whose are those eyes?"

"The sorcerer had put a spell on Hina," Tama replied without emotion. "He had to be punished."

"It was not a spell," Hina said, as though she had repeated it several times. "Someone hit me."

"Is he dead?" Kiyoyori said to Tama. "Master Sesshin?"

"No," she replied. "I told the truth. I spared his life and put him in the care of the last of the bandits, the young one."

"Shikanoko is his name," Hina said.

"I sent them both away." She looked calmly at him. "You would never have given them to the Prince Abbot, would you? Not even for our son's life."

"I was trying to buy time," he said. "I cannot be coerced, but while the Prince Abbot thinks I can, he will keep Tsumaru alive. However, you have left me with nothing to offer him."

"And you blame me?" she cried. "None of this is my fault! Look to your own actions!"

She had never raised her voice to him before and her accusation fueled his anger. He set guards at the doors to her rooms and took Hina to his own quarters. He wrestled, sleepless, with his thoughts, while Hina cried out in her dreams. He would kill his wife with his own hands; he would have her executed; he would force her to shave her head and become a nun.

He could hear the monks chanting all night as they kept vigil by the west gate. The next morning, a dull, cold day, threatening snow, Gessho let the werehawks out. They circled the roofs shrieking and then flew off toward the Darkwood.

"I will follow them," Gessho said. "There is nothing to be gained by waiting here. These others will return to Ryusonji and tell our master what has happened. You will hear from him in due course. In the meantime I would advise you to do nothing more to arouse his displeasure."

"If you find Sesshin and Shikanoko will my son be returned to me?" Kiyoyori asked.

"I cannot speak for my master," Gessho replied.

"I will come with you and help you find them."

Gessho brushed this offer away. "As I said, do nothing."

But this was the hardest thing to do, to wait day after day for news that never came. One moment he thought he must ride at once to the capital, the next that he must go in the other direction to Minatogura to press his own claim at Lord Miboshi Aritomo's famous tribunal. The thought of how his brother was undermining him in this way made his feelings toward Tama even colder, and he sought neither to comfort her nor to ask her advice. Sleeplessness made him irrational and his men began to fear the edge of his temper and question his judgment.

He had his wife confined to another pavilion, far out in the lake, accessible only by boat.

"You may have some items of worship," he said. "Spend your time in atonement."

Her serving women packed up two golden statues, and silks and needles for embroidery. Every day one or other of them was rowed out to take food and keep her company, but at night she was alone.

12

SHIKANOKO

Shikanoko and Sesshin stopped for a few hours on the stream's bank, huddled together for warmth. At dawn frost covered the blanket they shared and the horses' manes. They had nothing to eat and the water from the stream was so cold it made their teeth ache.

"Are you in pain?" Shika asked as he bathed the old man's face, carrying water in the flask the servant girl had thrust into his hands.

"Pain is a transient sensation. It will pass."

"I suppose hunger is, too, but I don't know if it is going to pass," Shika muttered.

"I will teach you to conquer both hunger and pain," Sesshin said, but his voice was faint.

The horses had cleared the ground of grass and were tearing at the tree bark. Shika saddled them and helped Sesshin onto Risu's back. He rode with his bow ready, but nothing stirred in the forest, no birds, no rabbits, not even a squirrel. The cedars gave way to ancient beeches and live oaks. Beneath the beeches lay the autumn mast in hard reddish pods. Shika dismounted and gathered handfuls, cracking them open in his teeth, but the kernels were thin and barely nourishing.

"Don't you have some magic that will tell us where to go or where to find something to eat?"

"My boy, I have suffered a setback. I need to learn the lesson it has for me before my powers revive."

"Should we return to Matsutani?" Shika wondered aloud. "Maybe Lord Kiyoyori will be back by now."

"We have been delivered from the Prince Abbot once. We should not put ourselves within his grasp again."

"Well, he certainly won't find us here! No one will even find our bones!"

Later that day, after they had left the stream and turned eastward, Shika, riding ahead, came on a small clearing and was able to shoot a rabbit before it reached the cover of the undergrowth. He made a fire and cooked the animal, feeding pieces to Sesshin. A little water had gathered among the roots of two trees twisted together. He helped Sesshin drink and lapped at it himself, until the horses pushed him away. The food made him thirstier. It was going to be another cold night.

"Can you hear water?" he said to Sesshin.

"I can hear a waterfall very far away."

"We must go at first light."

"I will teach you a water meditation," Sesshin said. "Once you master it you can go without water indefinitely."

"But can you teach it to the horses?"

Sesshin did not reply, but arranged himself, cross-legged on the ground, pulling the blanket around him.

After tethering the horses securely, Shika sat down next to him.

Sesshin said, "I sat under a waterfall for seven days and seven nights. The water entered my body and entered my bones and then my soul. I can call on it at any time." His voice droned on while within Shika thirst began to build unbearably. His throat burned, his mouth dried out, his lips were stretched taut and parched.

"Come close to me and place your mouth on mine," Sesshin said quietly.

Shika did so and a gush of cool water rushed into him, spilling over his lips.

I am dreaming, he thought, *I will awaken soon and be thirstier than ever.*

The flow of water stopped, his thirst was slaked, and suddenly sleep overwhelmed him.

The next morning, Sesshin was lethargic and feverish.

"I should not have done that," he said, rambling a little.

"The water thing? Can you do it again?"

"Not for a while. You can see how it's weakened me."

"Then we must ride on."

"Let's rest for a day or two until I get some strength back."

Shika studied the old man. "I'll take the horses up to the falls while you rest here. I'll come back."

"Very well. I won't be going anywhere."

Before he left he made a pile of firewood so Sesshin

could keep the fire alight. It was a steep climb up the ridge and took most of the day. Once he and the horses had reached the top and could see across the valleys, Shika realized where he was. The waterfall fell down the opposite cliff face, and the stream it formed flowed south toward Kumayama, his childhood home. To the north, beyond the mountains that lay in folds, violet in the evening light, was Shisoku's place. That would certainly be a refuge, but to get there he would have to fall down the cliff again. Still, knowing where he was made him feel better.

The horses caught the scent of water and began to scramble down the slope, crashing through the bushes and slipping on boulders. Shika clung to Nyorin's back, trusting him not to stumble.

Spray filled the air and the roar of the falls drowned out all other noise. The horses drank steadily. It was bitterly cold despite the winter sun, which had broken through the cloud cover and shone for a short while before dropping behind the mountains in the west. He would not get back before dark. The only vessel he had to carry water was the small bamboo flask. He found some roots of water plants, and a crab under a stone, and ate them both raw. Risu lay down and he settled beside her, his head on her belly. All night he was tormented by the idea of cutting her throat and drinking the warm blood. In the morning she looked at him reproachfully as though she knew what he was thinking.

He mounted Nyorin and set off back over the ridge. He shot and wounded a hare on the slope and spent some time tracking it down. It took longer to get back and darkness overtook him again before he came to the clearing. He could smell the smoke and see the flames. His heart swelled with relief. If the fire was still alight, Sesshin was probably still alive.

The old man stirred at Shika's approach but did not seem able to speak. Shika dripped some water into his mouth and set about skinning the hare. After feeding Sesshin he held him in his arms all night, trying to keep him warm. In the morning he seemed a little better, but still could not move.

The next day Shika let the horses go, still saddled, for there was no way he could carry their harness. He and Sesshin could share the water he had brought if they rationed themselves, but the horses had to drink. They grazed in the clearing for a while, keeping an eye on him, and then they wandered away. For a while he heard the noise of their progress through the woods, then silence returned. He hoped they would wait for him at the waterfall, but he couldn't help fearing he would not see them again.

Sesshin slowly recovered. Shika lost count of the days, but one afternoon Sesshin said, "I am sorry to have to tell you this, but someone is following us, guided by werehawks."

Shika listened, but could hear nothing beyond the usual sounds of the forest. A wood pigeon was calling monotonously and the wind rustled the beeches.

"How can you tell?"

"I heard twigs break, and the cry of the birds."

"How could you? I can't hear anything, with younger and sharper ears."

"Once I underwent a ritual that was meant to give me farsight, so I could see into distant places. It failed, for reasons connected with the nature of light, but when I recovered I found my hearing had increased a hundredfold. It was something of a burden—you may have noticed I used to plug my ears with wax—but now I am blind, it will prove very useful. This is why you should never concern yourself over your fate; everything follows the laws of destiny and therefore happens for a purpose."

"So, are we going to let this person, whoever it is, capture us, or is it our fate to escape?"

"I think we should make every effort not to be taken by one of the Prince Abbot's monks," Sesshin said, struggling to his feet. "I don't relish that prospect at all."

"But can you walk?"

"I will lean on your shoulder."

They made a slow, painful progress up the slope toward the top of the ridge. Shika could see where the horses had been before them, the broken branches where they had torn at leaves, their hoofprints in the soft earth. When they came to the summit he spotted Nyorin's white coat through the leaves below. They had found their way down to the waterfall and were still there. His heart filled with joy, and he let out a loud whistle. Nyorin whinnied in reply, echoed by the mare.

A bird shrieked above him.

"Hurry," Sesshin said. "They are here."

Pulling the old man after him, Shika half-slid, half-scrambled down the slope. The birds swooped over his head twice, then circled away, calling loudly. When they reached the bottom, Sesshin was trembling with fatigue. The horses trotted up to them, happy to see Shika. Risu's saddle had slipped around her belly and Nyorin had broken his reins. Shika quickly righted the saddle and lifted Sesshin onto the mare's back. He knotted the stallion's reins as best he could and swung himself up. There was no other way to go but downstream toward his old home, and in truth an irresistible longing had come over him to set eyes on it once more, before fleeing farther into the mountains.

The valley widened and slowly signs of human life began to appear. Irrigation ditches ran into small fields that lay fallow under vegetable waste and manure. In every corner stood trees, leafless now, but he knew each one, peach, loquat, mulberry. Smoke hung in the still air and its woody scent brought tears to his eyes. Not until this moment had he realized how much he had missed it all. His heart was thick with emotion and it made him careless.

"Look out!" Sesshin cried, at the same time as Shika heard the arrow whistling toward him and the shriek of the werehawks as they dived at his head. He pulled Risu close, dropped the lead rein, and sent her forward with a slap on her rump, then plucked an arrow from the quiver, brought Nyorin to a halt, and spun around. One of the werehawks raked his cheek with its beak, drawing blood.

A man was riding toward him, bow drawn, shouting in a voice so loud it echoed around the valley.

"I am the warrior monk Gessho, from Ryusonji! In the name of the Prince Abbot, surrender yourselves to me. I am commanded to bring you to him."

Shika tried to shoot toward him, but the werehawks flapped around his head, obscuring his sight; one seized the arrow in its claws and flew away with it. Nyorin, alarmed by the birds, gave a huge buck and bolted after Risu.

Another arrow whistled past Shika's head. They came to a fork in the track; the horses turned to the left and galloped into a group of armed men, led by Shika's uncle, Sademasa.

❊

Sademasa recognized him at once, Shika was sure. His uncle's face, beneath the elaborate horned helmet, paled as if he had seen a ghost. He thought the men also knew who he was, but they surrounded him with drawn swords, and he was afraid they would kill him and Sesshin without asking any questions.

"Uncle," he called out, as he calmed Nyorin. "It is I, Kazumaru." He reached out for Risu's rein and spoke softly to her. Both horses were breathing heavily. Sesshin turned his bandaged eyes toward the voices, listening carefully.

"My nephew is dead," Sademasa replied. "Who are you, imposter, and how dare you ride up to me with such an outrageous claim?"

"You know who I am. You were there when I fell off

the mountain a year ago. Lord Kiyoyori took me into his service."

"If you serve the Kuromori lord what are you doing here with this sightless beggar?"

Above their heads the werehawks were shrieking in triumph. The monk, who had named himself as Gessho, rode up, shouting. "Lower your swords. Do not harm these men. My lord, I am under orders from the Prince Abbot of Ryusonji to bring them directly to him, alive."

One of Sademasa's men said, "He does look like Kazumaru. What if it is him?" Shika knew him; his name was Naganori.

"Maybe he is a shape-shifter," Gessho declared, "who can take on the likeness of anyone, even the dead."

"I don't need to be a shape-shifter," Shika said. "I am Kazumaru. Naganori, I remember you. Your son, Nagatomo, was my friend."

The man's face lit up. "Lord Kazumaru . . ." he began, but Sademasa rode his horse forward, barging between Shika and Naganori, and addressed Gessho. "You can take them away. I'll send men with you to make sure they don't escape. As long as you remind your master of this service I am rendering him."

"You will indeed be rewarded," Gessho replied. "And even more if you provide us with shelter. It is too late to ride on today. Let us rest at your house and we will leave in the morning."

Shika glanced at Sesshin. If he had given one sign, made one gesture, Shika would have fought, no matter that he was outnumbered twenty to one. But Sesshin sat on the mare's back, calm and patient, as the warriors took the reins and led them away.

It was painful to return as a prisoner to his own home and to be shut in the guardroom, just inside the gate, where he had seen so many await punishment. Everything was taken from them, his bow and arrows, and the brocade bag that held the mask, which Gessho, who seemed reluctant to let his captives out of his sight, received with delight and awe and said many prayers over.

"This will please my master," he exclaimed, opening it enough to peer inside.

"What is it?" Sademasa said, curious, but Gessho would not show him.

Until then Shika had kept his feelings under control, but when the mask was taken from him he flew into a rage just as he used to when he was a boy. It took three men to restrain him. He was still raging when the guard returned with a bowl of gruel, and would have thrown it in the man's face, but Sesshin's voice calmed him. "It is food. Eat. Isn't that what you wanted?"

"None of this is what I wanted," he said, but he ate the gruel. He lay awake all night, vowing he would take revenge on his uncle and reclaim what was his.

✻

There was no sign of the horses when they were brought out next morning, and Shika was afraid he would never see them again. The rage that he had kept simmering all night threatened to erupt once more. His uncle had stolen everything from him, even his horses.

Gessho said, "Bring the horses. The prisoners can ride the mare, and the stallion will make a fine gift for my lord, the Prince Abbot."

Sademasa, who had come out to bid farewell to the monk, said, "We cannot get near them. One of my men has been bitten on the arm and another kicked in the head. I will have them killed. They will feed my men through the winter."

"Untie the young prisoner," Gessho said, after a moment's thought. "Walk with me to the stables," he said quietly to Shika.

A group of men followed them, bows ready, swords drawn.

"Don't try to escape," Gessho said under his breath. "Sademasa will seize any pretext to kill you."

Shika realized it was less a threat than a warning. He looked at the warrior monk, seeing him properly for the first time. He was tall and broad shouldered, with well-shaped features and almost copper-colored skin. He carried a rattan-bound bow and a quiver of arrows fletched with black-banded eagle feathers. He had a long sword at his hip. Even if Shika had his own bow, and the mask, he did not think he could take on a man the size of Gessho.

The horses had been left in a small fenced area. The ground was churned up by their hoofs and they were wild eyed and sweating despite the cold. They whinnied in relief at the sight of Shika. They were both still saddled and bridled from the previous night, and though they had been given food and water, they had been too agitated to eat. Shika ran his hand over the stallion's flanks. He had lost weight during their flight over the mountains and his mane was tangled, his coat dirty.

He led Nyorin forward and Risu followed docilely, her head at Shika's shoulder.

Sademasa's men encircled them, but Gessho had his hand on his sword and they fell back to let them through. Shika hoisted the old man onto Risu's back and then looked at Gessho.

"You may as well ride the stallion," the monk said. "Since it seems no one else can. But I will tie him to my horse."

"Where are the werehawks?" Shika said, looking up. The clouds had cleared and the sun was shining from a pale sky.

"I sent them back to the capital," Gessho replied. "My lord Abbot will know I have accomplished my task and will dispatch men to meet us."

Shika's heart twisted as they rode away from his home. No one looked at him, no one recognized him as the young lord of Kumayama. Yet he knew every tree, the pattern of their winter shadows, the outline of the mountains rising one behind the other, ever higher, to the snowcapped peaks, sharp and gleaming in the frosty air——they were all as familiar as his own hands.

At the boundary of his land Gessho told Sademasa's men to return home. They obeyed him——he was the sort of man, Shika realized, that would always be obeyed; as well as his gigantic build and strength he had powerful spiritual authority. After they had gone, Gessho said, "Lord Sademasa seems eager to get rid of you. Why should he be, unless your claim is true? That's what I've been asking myself."

"It is true," Shika said. "Last year I fell while we were out hunting. I believe he tried to kill me then—but whatever his intentions, he certainly left me for dead."

"Did his men not recognize you?"

"At least one of them did."

"Yet none of them came to your aid and most of them were prepared to take your life. He must rule his little domain with an iron hand and a cruel will. They are all afraid of him. He is Lord Kiyoyori's vassal, I believe. Are you?"

"I don't know," Shika replied. "We always served the Kuromori lords, and Lord Kiyoyori spared my life and took me into his household. But he was in two minds about it since my uncle, he said, is one of his staunchest allies."

"Indeed. Just as Kuromori protects the capital, so it is itself protected by Kumayama."

When Shika made no response, Gessho said, "I don't know what my master, the Prince Abbot, intends to do with you, but he rewards those who serve him well. Maybe one day your estate will be restored to you."

It will, Shika promised himself.

※

Sesshin said very little on the journey. He seemed to have withdrawn inside himself. He made no complaints, though his body alternately burned with fever and shivered as though it would never be warm again. Shika tended to all his needs, washed him and tried to feed him, though the old man would take hardly more than a mouthful of broth or hot water. From time to time he pressed Shika's hand in thanks. He did not speak to Gessho. Often his lips moved as if in prayer.

They followed the course of the Kumagawa as it flowed toward the sea. The river was fast and shallow, splashing over rocks and boulders, its noise constantly in their ears. The first night, they came to the high road that ran along the coast between Miyako and Minatogura, and stopped at a small place on the corner. From here on there were a few scattered villages along the road, with stalls that supplied food and drink, wooden clogs, fur boots, cloths, and other traveling needs, and one or two lodging places. After the first night, they did not stay at these but at temples that belonged to Ryusonji and where the dragon child was worshipped. The rooms were austere and cold, the food meager. The monks rose at midnight, and the dark hours till morning echoed with their chanting and the dull reverberation of gongs and bells.

On the third morning they came to a crossroads. To the south lay a small seaport where vessels plied between Akashi and Minatogura and fishermen went out to the islands of the Encircled Sea. On the northern road two partially decomposed heads had been placed on stakes. Crows flapped around them, pecking at the rotting flesh. The eyes had been taken and the teeth were beginning their eternal grin. They were beyond recognition yet Shika knew them, remembered hearing them fall, when he thought his own would follow them.

"That is the road to Matsutani," Gessho said. "But we will not be going there."

"Is Lord Kiyoyori there?" Shika asked.

"That is no longer a concern of yours," Gessho replied.

Every morning Sesshin seemed smaller, as though he were withering away. Not only physically: some inner light was fading from him. He was becoming an empty husk, an old bean pod ready for fire or earth.

Gessho never left them alone and at night tied their hands and feet, but even monks have to obey the call of nature, and the day they were to arrive at the capital, before he untied them, he went off to the privy at the back of the temple where they had stayed for the night. Sesshin spoke for the first time in days.

"Shikanoko! Come here, my boy. I must pass something over to you. Quickly, there is very little time."

"What is it?"

"Remember the night you drank from my mouth? I have another gift for you. If I don't give it to you the Prince Abbot will take it from me. Come, place your mouth over mine."

"What is it?" Shika said again.

"It is my power. I have concentrated it down into—well, into a sort of pellet. Take it inside you. It will grow like a seed. But be quick."

Shika rolled over to the old man's side and placed his mouth over the other's, tasting the fever and the decaying flesh. Then he felt a smooth, hard object on his tongue. Its flavor was sweet and fiery, bitter beyond words and smooth as honey at the same time. For a moment he thought he would gag on it, but it slipped down his throat and, like wine, spread instantly. He felt hot and cold all at once. The fires of earth rushed from his feet upward through his body, where they crashed hissing into the freezing snows of heaven that fell through his skull. His limbs bucked against the ties, throbbing. Snakes swam through his veins. A catlike animal purred in his brain. His skin sweated drops of ice.

He lay panting. Sesshin rested his brow against Shika's cheek. "Good," he whispered. "I was afraid it might be too strong and would tear you apart. Don't do anything for a while. Just let it grow." He began to speak more hurriedly. "There is one more thing I must tell you. About Lady Tora."

"She did not die in the fire?" Shika questioned, astonished as well as relieved.

"She escaped and has gone to the sorcerer in the mountains. She took something from me, and from you and Lord Kiyoyori, and from two others, I am not sure who they were. Maybe that bandit chief, and the old sorcerer himself. She needed it to make her children. From five fathers, five children will be born. Find them and destroy them. They will be demons. She is one of the Old People. I should never have succumbed to her. No wonder all these disasters followed. Well, I can do nothing about it now—but you can. You have shown me you have a kind heart despite your rough appearance and your bad temper. Don't be kind to the demons."

Gessho returned with food and untied their bonds. As they approached the capital the meals had become more refined and flavorsome. This morning they had rice with grilled fish and pickled radish. For the first time, Sesshin ate healthily. Gessho peered at him with suspicion.

"What's happened? He looks different."

"Perhaps he is feeling better," Shika said.

"I am the same as when you met me," Sesshin said. "A harmless old man, preparing to pass over to the next world, blinded for no reason by a poor woman driven mad by grief."

A new merriment had come over him, and indeed he seemed exactly what he said he was: an old man, joyful and serene at the end of his life.

Gessho ground his teeth in exasperation and, without giving them time to finish the meal, called for the horses. They set out immediately, riding at a gallop toward the capital.

❋

They arrived at Ryusonji late in the evening. Guided by the Prince Abbot's men who had come to meet them, they did not ride along the wide avenues of Miyako but skirted through the hills of the northeast, passing many temples lit up by a thousand candles and oil lamps and echoing with the endless sutras that bound earth to Heaven and kept the city safe.

The temple of Ryusonji lay a little way to the north of the capital, near the riverbank. In the low-lying ground between the temple and the river was the lake where the dragon child dwelled. As they passed through the great main gate and into the first courtyard, snow began to fall, making swirling patterns in the torch lights.

The horses, too exhausted to protest, were handed over to grooms, and Shika and Sesshin were taken to an outdoor hot spring where the dirt of the journey was scrubbed from them. They were purified with incense and dressed in old robes of bleached hemp, patched and darned but spotlessly clean. Shika's hair was untied, washed, combed, and tied up again. All this was carried out by low-rank monks who worked silently and carefully with no sign of emotion, neither hate nor fear. Then Shika and Sesshin were led through a series of corridors and courtyards under great gates and through dark halls where carved images of the gods of Hell, saints, avatars, and the Enlightened One himself glimmered faintly, until they came at last to the rooms of the Prince Abbot.

As the door slid open Shika saw Gessho was waiting inside. He had changed from his armor and traveling attire into temple robes. Silently and with an impassive face he put his hand on Shika's neck and forced him to his knees. Shika lowered his head to the ground and remained there for several minutes. He heard Sesshin say cheerfully, "Ah, it's good to be clean. All thanks to you, mighty priest, whoever you are. Truly you follow the teachings of the Enlightened One. Your worship could be in the paradise of the pure land, but you have chosen to remain in this world and relieve the sufferings of the afflicted, as did the holy Jizo," and he went prattling on, praising the Prince Abbot and recounting the lives and miracles of holy men. Finally his voice dwindled away and he sat nodding and smiling.

The Prince Abbot spoke to Gessho. "What happened?"

"My lord, his eyes had been put out before we arrived. The Matsutani lady's anger was inflamed against him— she suspected him of involvement in the disappearance of her son. He and this young man had been turned out into the Darkwood. There was a woman whom Lady Matsu-tani accused of being a sorceress, though her judgment may have been clouded by jealousy, as the said woman was Lord Kiyoyori's concubine. She apparently burned to death in the fire that consumed the old man's books and instruments. I left Kiyoyori to deal with his wife and followed these two, catching up with them at Kumayama, where the local lord, Jiro no Sademasa, was of some assis-tance. I said you would reward him, by the way. He was eager to get rid of the young man, who it seems could be the nephew who was believed to be dead—you may remember?"

"Interesting. I do remember and we will come to that by and by. First I must consider my old friend here, Mas-ter Sesshin. We were novices together many years ago. Sesshin excelled in esoteric practices and eventually chose the way of a mountain hermit. I had not set eyes on him for years, but from time to time I heard of some miracle, some challenge to the unseen powers, and knew it must be him. He would surface and then disappear. I tried to keep an eye on him, but he vanished for many years until something drew my attention to Matsutani and there he was! So it was your power at work, behind Kiyoyori, all this time?"

"Your Holiness must be confusing me with someone else," Sesshin said. "I knew all this attention was too good to be true. Well, that is the wheel of life. We all must pay for our misdeeds from past lives."

"I am sorry, my lord Abbot," Gessho said. "I could not get him to you quickly enough. It was as if some change took place in him on the road. One moment you could see that despite his suffering he was a powerful sage; the next he had become this old fool."

"What a pathetic end to our years of rivalry," the Abbot said. "Why did you not fight like a warrior of the spirit? I have dreamed of confronting you most of my life. Is this what you have become?"

Sesshin smiled and nodded. "I am what I am and what I have always been, a poor soul on a journey."

"Is he genuine, my lord, or a very good actor?" Gessho said doubtfully.

"I sense nothing in him, no depth, no secrets. If he had any power he has divested himself of it utterly. We will keep him for a while and watch him. Treat him well, keep him occupied."

"Perhaps he could join the blind lute player and the singers," Gessho suggested.

"Ah, music." Sesshin gave a deep sigh. "To devote my final years to music, under the protection of the mighty Prince Abbot, in the holy precinct of Ryusonji! It is more than I could have dreamed of."

Shika, by turning his head slightly, could see the Prince Abbot's disconcerted expression. One of the monks took Sesshin away. After a few moments he heard the priest's voice telling him to sit up and come closer. He shuffled forward on his knees.

"So, this is my young stag?" The Abbot placed his hands on Shika's head, gazed into his eyes and touched the side of his face, almost like a caress. Shika could not help trembling. He remembered the gaze and heard again Sesshin's voice, *Don't speak*. He lowered his eyes and remained silent.

"Well, you are pleasing enough to look at. I don't mind keeping you by my side for a while. Especially if you will show me the use of this lovely thing."

He made a sign to one of the young monks who knelt behind him and the man stepped forward holding out the seven-layered brocade bag. The Prince Abbot drew out the mask. As always Shika felt a rush of pleasure at the sight of it, the long black lashes, the cinnabar-colored lips, the polished antlers, the memory of its making, the knowledge of its power.

"Where did you come by this? Who made it for you?"

He did not reply immediately and then a false memory

began to create itself in his mind. He saw himself coming upon the mask. It was half-buried in sandy ground, on the riverbank.

"I found it. It must have been washed downstream after a flood."

"You found it and then dared to use it? Just like that? Even I have not dared do that."

"I thought it was mine because I found it."

"That is a dangerous idea. Let's see what happens if just anyone puts it on." The Abbot beckoned to the young monk without turning and held the mask out to him. "Put it on."

"Don't!" Shika said, suddenly knowing what was going to happen. "He should not!"

The monk was very handsome, with fine, regular features and smooth, almost golden skin. He hesitated for a moment and then put the mask to his face.

Immediately he began screaming. He tried to take the mask off, his hands tearing vainly at it, but it clung to him. Gessho ran forward to help him, holding him still, pulling with all his great strength, but with no success. The young man broke away from him, shouting and crying. He rammed his head against the wall, and then, falling, on the floor. The Abbot stood, a movement shocking in itself, and stretched out his hand, speaking solemn words of power that unlocked rocks and summoned the dead back to life, but nothing shifted the mask until Shika went to the writhing figure and touched the polished surface. It slid into his hand. It was burning hot; it had only ever felt cool before. He felt its distress, its panic and pain, the fall from the cliff, the broken leg, the cut throat, the ebbing blood. *Nothing is ever lost*, it whispered to him. *It changes and takes a new form. All suffering mutates and persists.*

The young monk stared up at them. The skin of his face was stripped as if he had fallen into a fire, eyebrows and eyelashes singed away, cheeks seared purple, lips blistered. He wept helpless tears.

"Eisei, my poor boy, forgive me," the Prince Abbot cried. "I did not know it would be so extreme."

Even Gessho looked shaken. "Your Holiness might have tried it. What would have happened then?"

"Take Eisei away and tend to him," the Prince Abbot said, his voice unsteady with shock. When the monks had done this he asked Gessho, "Who still wields this ancient forest magic?"

"I don't know. I have never seen such a thing."

The Prince Abbot handed the brocade bag to Shika and watched him put the mask away.

"This is what I think happened, Kazumaru—do you still call yourself that?"

"Now my name is Shikanoko," Shika replied.

"Of course. The deer's child. As I was saying, you disappeared a year ago and during that time you met a mountain sorcerer who corrupted you with dark magic. He made you the mask from the skull of a stag, perhaps one you had killed, a wise old creature that bequeathed its power to you. But who else was involved? This mask has female power as well as male. Who was the woman? Was it the

same one who bewitched Kiyoyori? That would be fasci-
nating beyond words. Where is she now?"

"As Gessho said, she burned to death," Shikanoko said,
disturbed by the accuracy of the Prince Abbot's insights.

"If that is true, we have nothing to worry about. But if
she escaped, it might be a cause for concern. This is a very
powerful object."

Shikanoko felt the power latent within him but had no
idea what to do with it. There was something very attractive, almost calming, about the priest's acknowledgment
of the mask.

The Prince Abbot studied him with shrewd eyes as if
he could read his mind.

"You do understand that I must take control of this
sort of sorcery? We will find its author in the spring. In the
meantime you will stay with me. Together we will discover
exactly how much you know and what can be done with
the mask. In return I will restore Kumayama to you. We
will send a claim to the Miboshi and it will be confirmed
in the courts of justice in Minatogura. In the coming war
your uncle will be overthrown along with the Kuromori
lord and all the Kakizuki."

Somewhere in the distance a cock crowed, followed
by another. A bell began to toll from the innermost hall of
the temple.

"My lord, it is nearly dawn," Gessho said.

"You may tell me your decision when we meet again.
Give me the mask. I will take great care of it. I know you
will not leave without it."

"And if I refuse to cooperate with you?" Shika said as he reluctantly handed it over.

"You will be put to death and the mask will be destroyed. That will be your uncle's reward. But I don't believe you are willing to die yet."

Gessho took him to a small room, where a thin mat lay on the wooden boards, and told him to lie down. Despite his exhaustion Shika could not sleep. Somewhere the bell tolled again and he heard the pad of feet as the monks assembled for prayer. He saw again the young monk's ruined face and felt the terror and power of the mask. He realized with some fear how little he knew of it or how to control it. Deep within him something—whatever it was that Sesshin had transmitted to him—continued to quiver. It had to be kept hidden, but he had to learn how to use it. He knew the Prince Abbot was right. He was not yet willing to die, and he could not bear the thought that the mask would be destroyed. And part of him was already under the sway of the Prince Abbot's seductive personality. The priest's attention and interest reassured and flattered him.

Shika had just come to the conclusion that he had nowhere else to go when he fell into a deep slumber, only to be woken abruptly after what felt like mere minutes. It was morning; a gray snowy light filled the room.

A monk was shaking him. "Get up! Our lord Abbot wishes to speak to you."

The Prince Abbot sat in the same room, with the same monks around him, apart from the young man whom the mask had burned. Previously he had hidden his unease beneath an air of calm, but now he let Shika see his rage.

"You are already working against me? You dared to strike, taking advantage of my lenience and generosity?"

"My lord?" he said.

"How did you do it? How did you spirit the boy away?"

"I don't understand. I thought about what I should do and then I fell asleep. How could I do anything else? Your Holiness has the mask. I was alone with your men watching me all night. Anyway, what boy are you talking about?"

"Kiyoyori's son."

Shika could not hide his surprise. "You had Tsumaru? It was you who took him?"

"I had him brought here. I thought to persuade his father to send you and the old man to me. Now that I have you in my hands I intended to return him, but while I was occupied with questioning you last night, someone stole him away."

"It was not I," Shika said.

"You did not perform some magic that made the guards' eyes sightless or the boy invisible?"

"I have no idea how to do such things! Did you think I could?"

The Prince Abbot leaned forward and studied him. "Well, I believe you. And I think you are capable of more than you have ever dreamed. That will be our work together. I take it you have agreed to serve me?"

It was this, not the threats or the promise of Kumayama

or the granting of his life, but his desire to harness this power, that persuaded Shikanoko to become the Prince Abbot's disciple in Ryusonji that winter, while ice froze the lake and the river, and snow blanketed the capital and the mountains.

13

TAMA

The island pavilion had been designed by Tama's mother, a retreat on hot summer days, filled with poetry, music, and laughter. It had been Tama's favorite place when she was a girl. Now it had been her cold, damp prison all winter. Every day she listened for her son's voice, for some sign that he had been returned alive, but as the weeks went by she began to feel she would never see him again. Often she wept in grief and rage, but only the guards who kept watch outside on the tiny veranda all night heard her, and they were unmoved.

One morning, early in the new year, after the snow melted, she was woken at dawn by an earthquake. It growled like an angry beast approaching from afar, its roar growing louder and louder. The doors and screens rattled. A shutter broke loose and began banging like a drum. There were cries and shouts as the household awoke, the neighing of startled horses and frantic barking of dogs.

The guards took the boat and poled back to the shore. She watched them leave, saw the boat ground halfway to the shore, noticed the sudden flow of water toward the lake's outlet in the southeast. She dressed quickly, hiding her prayer beads in her sleeve and slipping the golden statues into a small bag. Her dagger she kept on her day and night, hidden under her clothes. By this time the water had receded even more. Stranded fish were flapping and struggling in the mud and stones of the lake floor. The rock wall that contained it had cracked and the water was pouring through it.

Tama walked away from her island prison leaving delicate footsteps in the mud like a fox woman's. Fire had broken out in the stables and the main residence and in the confusion no one saw her go.

Houses were destroyed all the way to the coast. Tama became one of the many homeless people seeking refuge, and at the port of Shimaura she traded one of the statues for a berth on a temple ship, bound for Minatogura.

The winds were fresh from the southwest and the sea rough. Many passengers were afflicted with seasickness, but Tama, even though she had never been on a ship before, felt as well as she ever had in her life, filled with a sense of freedom and excitement. She stood on deck hardly noticing the cold, watching the pine-covered islands, dotted here and there with the vermilion posts of a shrine. Sometimes they passed by close enough to see fragile white blossoms on the plum trees.

A group of women who were going on a pilgrimage befriended her. One of them had already shaved her head and was about to enter the convent at Muenji.

"It was founded by Miboshi Aritomo's wife, Lady Masa, before she died, as a refuge for widows and other women: some are fleeing from violent husbands, some have been turned out of their own land and are seeking justice from the Miboshi, some, like me, simply want to retire from the world and find peace and grace before death."

"I am seeking justice," Tama said. "My first husband lives in Minatogura and serves the Miboshi. I was forced to leave him and marry his older brother, one of the Kakizuki. He treated me very badly, took over the estate I inherited from my family, and kept me a prisoner. I want to recover what is mine."

"Including your rightful husband, I suppose," said Jun, the woman who was going to become a nun.

"I long for him day and night," Tama said. "I have never stopped longing for him. Also, my son was kidnapped and I have not seen him all winter. I don't know if he is alive or dead. I need someone to intercede for me."

The women sighed in sympathy and wet their sleeves with their tears. Plovers cried mournfully from the shore.

"How pitiful," Jun said. "Come with us to Muenji and we will take care of you and support your cause."

Tama watched the moon rise and set, seeing how it grew fuller every night, and on the fifth morning they came to the great port city where the Miboshi family held sway.

The women's temple was a little way out of town on the top of a hill overlooking the port. To the south lay the Encircled Sea, to the east the vast ocean where huge whales spouted and beyond which, in distant lands, men the size of giants hunted seals and wolves. Tama had been to the capital, Miyako, a few times, but Minatogura seemed even larger, and, from her vantage point on the hill, she could see clearly that it was a town preparing for war. Warriors thronged the streets, long horse lines stretched in every open space, armorers, fletchers, and swordsmiths worked day and night, their fires blazing, their hammers ringing. Straw targets were set up in gardens and on the riverbank and the angry whining of bulb-ended humming arrows filled the air. Flags and banners fluttered everywhere in the dazzling white of the Miboshi clan.

At Muenji, Tama was given shelter. Jun related her story to the Abbess, and Tama was duly summoned and interrogated by a slender, graceful woman, much younger than Tama had expected. She thought the Abbess must be a former noblewoman; she had obviously been well educated, could read and write, and had a careful and astute intelligence. She promised to make inquiries, and a few days later Tama was called once again to her room.

"I have verified all you told me and have discovered your husband is living at the house of Yamada Saburo Keisaku, his father's cousin. Masachika has become his adopted son and is to marry Keisaku's daughter, as soon as she is old enough."

"He is to marry her?" Tama felt weak with shock.

"Well, take courage. He is not married yet. He is, however, claiming the estate, currently held by his older brother, which you say is yours."

"Matsutani. It is my family home. After my brother's

death, it was given to me, and my husband—without me what right does either of them have?"

"They have the right of being male," the Abbess said drily. "Whose idea was it to wrench you from one brother and give you to another?"

"Their father's, but mine agreed to it."

"I hope they are both atoning in Hell for their blind, arrogant wickedness. But what do you want to do next?"

"I want Masachika back, I want my land, and I want to know if my son is alive or dead," Tama said.

"Where is your son now?"

"He was taken as a hostage to Ryusonji. I don't really understand why. My husband, Kiyoyori, became involved in sorcery, with a woman. The Prince Abbot learned about it and wanted to bend Kiyoyori to his will. But Kiyoyori would never be swayed like that. He would sooner let his son die. I thought, if someone from the Miboshi were to approach the Prince Abbot, he might return Tsumaru to me, if he is still alive."

"Is he your only child?"

"There is a stepdaughter, Hina. She has always been cold toward me. Her father spoils her, because she reminds him of his wife who died."

The Abbess looked at Tama with her shrewd eyes. "Are you sure you are not misjudging Lord Kiyoyori? Is no reconciliation possible? It is my duty to ask you this. The bonds between husband and wife spring from deep laws of destiny and should not be broken lightly."

"I seek to restore a bond that was broken," Tama said. "The one with my original husband."

"I will send a message to him," the Abbess said.

Tama joined in the activities of the convent while she waited nervously, but even in prayer and meditation among the calm-eyed women her mind would not be still. She had not seen Masachika for seven years. She had aged, she had borne a child. Would he remember the young girl she had been, their nights of sweetness?

Two days later, around midday, Jun came and told her to walk in the garden, the outer one where visitors were permitted. She saw three horses outside the gate and two men waiting for him. So, he was already within somewhere.

Her heart was beating uncontrollably as she walked along the stone path toward a small thatched hut that overlooked the lake. It was a bright spring day though the wind came from the east, giving a chill to the air. Cherry trees surrounded the lake, pink-budded but still a week from full flowering.

Masachika stood at the entrance to the hut. She studied him greedily. His clothes were new and made of fine silk; he wore a small black hat on his head. He had filled out; he was fully a man now, both like and unlike his older brother, taller and more handsome.

At the end of the path, boulders formed a step and yellow flowers blossomed between them. She caught their fragrance as she fell to her knees.

"Lord Masachika! My husband!"

He bent and lifted her by both hands and guided her into the interior. Then she was in his arms, remembering his smell, his hair, his skin. Neither of them spoke.

Finally he released her. They sat side by side on silk cushions. He said, "Why are you here? Is my brother dead?"

"No, although, forgive me for saying it, I have wished many times he were. Terrible events occurred at Matsutani. He imprisoned me all winter. There was an earthquake and I ran away." When he said nothing, Tama went on. "I know you were in contact with some of our old retainers— Enryo and his wife."

"Kiyoyori had them killed, I believe," Masachika said.

"Somehow he was forewarned that he would be ambushed in the hunt. He made Enryo ride his horse and take the arrow that was intended for him." She remembered the desperate woman running. "His wife tried to stop the attack. She was tortured to death."

"He has become cruel," Masachika observed.

"Cruel and selfish. There is—was—a woman, too. She was a sorceress, and so was the old man." Tama could hear her voice rising and stopped abruptly.

"What old man? Calm down, tell me slowly."

"Master Sesshin."

"My grandfather's friend? Is he still alive?"

She told him everything; he asked many questions, and when her account was completed he sat gazing at the lake, deep in thought.

Tama said, hearing the pleading in her voice and despising it, "In my mind and spirit I never stopped being your wife."

"Seven years is a long time and a lot has happened." Masachika did not look at her. "I was sent away against my will, but I have found a good life here. I am grateful now to my father for allying me with the Miboshi, with the side who are going to be the victors. My adoptive father is a fine man, very wealthy. He has treated me generously and I am betrothed to his daughter."

"But I was told she is only a child! She cannot give you what I once gave you, and will give you again, now, here, if you want."

He tried to joke. "You would cause the poor nuns some distress."

Tama plunged on. "You will take me to your home? We can live together? If only you knew how I have longed for you. Haven't you longed for me?"

"When we were separated," Masachika said quietly, "it was as though a limb had been wrenched from me. It would have been easier to bear if you had died. I would not have had to endure imagining you in my brother's arms, with all the pain and humiliation that brought me. I hated him more than I would have thought possible, and when I heard you had given him a son I hated you, too." He gave her a quick glance and then resumed his study of the lake.

"What could I do? I was helpless."

"I thought you should have killed yourself with your mother's dagger rather than submit to him."

"I thought of it," Tama said, "and I thought about killing him, too. But I had the estate to look after. I had Matsutani."

He shifted uncomfortably. "You know I have made a claim to the estate in the judicial court here? The Miboshi set a great store by legality. Moreover, everyone knows Matsutani is the gateway to Miyako. It's no secret that the Miboshi intend to move against the capital. If Kiyoyori will not submit to the verdict of law, the Miboshi will support me in taking up arms against him and winning the estate in battle. They will have a staunch ally in a key position and I will have what was mine."

"Your claim will be all the stronger if I am your wife," Tama said. "After all, it is my family who have owned Matsutani for generations." He was making her uneasy. She wished he had not said he hated her. She was afraid he would no longer want her, now Kiyoyori's flesh had been imprinted on hers and contained within her.

"I am committed elsewhere," he said. "I can't easily escape from that commitment."

"But, as I said, she is only a child."

"When we were first betrothed she was seven years old. I have watched her grow up and waited for her. Next year she will turn fifteen."

Fifteen, Tama thought, *the age I was when I was betrothed to him.* Jealousy and misery welled up in her heart. No wonder he was reluctant to take her back. He would have both Matsutani and his young bride, and increased standing and respect among the Miboshi.

"Let's be patient," Masachika said. "Nothing will be achieved by acting in haste. Let's see how the court case is resolved. In the meantime you can stay here, I suppose?"

"Can you help me? I should have a waiting-woman, I

will need new clothes, and of course I should make a donation to the convent."

"It would be a little difficult," Masachika said. "I would have to ask my parents, and I think it is better if they don't know you are in Minatogura."

"But how long will I have to wait?"

"The court case will be heard before the end of the month."

❋

"He will not take me back," Tama said later to the Abbess. "I was a fool to expect it. Maybe I was a fool to come here, but what else could I do? I could not stay where I was, a prisoner in my own home, waiting for my husband to get rid of me. And I cannot go back to Matsutani unless . . ." She fell silent.

"Unless what?" the older woman prompted.

"Unless the Miboshi's famous justice system confirms me as the rightful owner. Why should I not also submit a claim?"

"It is possible," the Abbess said after a moment's reflection. "There are precedents."

"Matsutani is a prosperous estate. I will be able to endow this convent for years to come. You must have important connections; you can advise me on how to set about it."

The Abbess smiled slightly. "Presumably you have documents recording your family's history?"

"Of course," Tama said, "unless they were destroyed in

the earthquake, they are all there. Kiyoyori has copies, but the originals are hidden in a place known only to me. I could send someone to get them . . . I would need a skillful thief."

She looked at the Abbess. The other woman said, "I'm afraid I have none in my acquaintance. Let us pray and meditate on how to proceed in these matters. I will give you my decision tomorrow."

❋

The following day the Abbess decided that the convent would support Tama's claim and a request was sent to the tribunal for permission to proceed. Then a long time passed in which she heard nothing. She was used to the constant activity of running a large estate; with nothing to occupy her, her mind buzzed with regrets for the past and plans for the future. Despite her words about Masachika to the Abbess and against her own better judgment, she could not help hoping and dreaming. She believed from the way he had held her that Masachika still loved her as she knew she still loved him. But the pretty features of a fifteen-year-old she had never met haunted her. If only she could regain Matsutani surely Masachika would return to her. If she had the support of the Miboshi maybe Tsumaru would be rescued. She was on the point of deciding she would go back to Matsutani to collect the documents herself when she was told the Abbess wanted to see her. She went at once to the tranquil room near the front entrance of the convent.

The Abbess led her quietly to the side veranda where they could see the gate, and indicated a waiting man.

"Is that someone you know? He says he comes from Matsutani with a message from Lord Kiyoyori."

Her heart plummeted. It could only be news of Tsumaru. But she did not recognize the man. Kiyoyori would surely have sent one of his senior retainers, Sadaike or Tsuneto. But Kiyoyori did not know where she was—no one knew except Masachika. Could he have sent this man to her, with some message, some promise? But why pretend to be from Matsutani?

"I've never seen him," she whispered, as though he could hear her. "I don't believe Kiyoyori sent him."

"Then I will have him turned away," the Abbess declared.

"No, he can only have been sent by Masachika. I must hear what he has to say."

"My dear." The Abbess gave her a pitying look. "What if his purpose is more brutal than a mere message?"

"What do you mean? That Masachika would have me murdered?" Tama did not know whether to laugh or cry.

"Well, you are threatening to come between him and his estate."

After a few moments in which she regained her composure, Tama said, "If you turn him away we won't know for sure who sent him or if he might not strike again. Let him in and I'll give him a welcome he won't expect."

"Be careful. We must avoid shedding blood. I will bring him to you myself."

She waited for him in the same hut where she had met Masachika. She had her knife in her hand and had placed a halberd just inside the entrance. The man must have been lulled by the calm of the courtyards and gardens through which he had been escorted, as much as by the presence of the Abbess, for he stepped from the bright daylight into the darkness without hesitation. She had her knife at his throat before he had even seen her, and when he lunged backward, twisting away from her, he found himself up against the sharp blade of the halberd in the hands of the Abbess.

"Don't move!" said the Abbess. "We don't want to have to kill you."

The man fell to his knees. "Forgive me," he cried. "I should never have come here."

"Reveal the weapons you are carrying," Tama said. "Then I'll decide what to do with you."

When he did not answer immediately, she put the knife to his throat again, the sharp blade piercing the skin.

He cried out.

"It's nothing," she said, holding the knife steady. "Not even a flesh wound. But don't misunderstand me. I will let your life blood out in an instant."

He said, "I left my sword at the gate. I am unarmed."

"You are lying. I think you came to kill me. Were you going to strangle me with your bare hands?"

"I carry one hidden blade. In the breast of my jacket I have a leather garotte, in the sleeve wax pellets that contain poison."

"Is that all?" Tama said, swiftly locating each one. "What about these?" She had located a tiny blowpipe and a set of darts in a miniature quiver. There was something almost intimate about searching him. Suddenly she was aware of him as a man.

"Take care," he said, "they are fatally poisonous."

She heard real concern in his voice and realized with a flash of amusement that he found her attractive, that the situation pleased him.

"You thought to murder me," she said. "You say you come from Matsutani with a message from Lord Kiyoyori?"

"It was not he who sent me," the man admitted.

"I know that. For a start he does not know I am here, and he would never send an assassin to murder his wife in secret; he would come here and kill me himself. He would do me that honor. He and I may have parted, we may hate each other, but I hope we do not despise each other." Her voice deepened with emotion. "It can only have been the one other person who knows where I am, Masachika."

"I am sorry," he said. "It was indeed Lord Masachika. I am employed by his family."

"Really?" Tama's tone was scathing. "Do they often send you on such missions? Killing defenseless women in convents? Is that the honorable way among the warriors of the east? Let me look at you."

The Abbess raised the blinds on the western side and the evening light filled the room. Then she took up the halberd again.

Tama said, "I am going to lower the knife now."

He instinctively put up his hand to wipe away the blood.

"Don't move!" she said. She moved around to face him and studied him for a moment. "You seem to be a man of many talents," she observed.

He fell to his knees and bowed to the ground. "Lady, my name is Hisoku. All my talents are yours to command. I beg you to allow me to serve you."

"Any man will make such vows at the wrong end of a halberd," she replied. "You were sent to kill me. Why should I believe your sudden change of heart?"

"I can hardly believe it myself," he said, raising his head. "I cannot explain it. I feel you have saved me from a terrible sin. If I had killed you I would never be able to atone for it. But now in your service perhaps I will find forgiveness."

Tama turned to the older woman. "My lady Abbess, do you think he is sincere?"

The Abbess gave the halberd to Tama to hold and knelt before Hisoku. She gazed into Hisoku's eyes and then her own eyes closed and an intense silence fell on the room. From the garden a bush warbler called, the first Tama had heard that spring.

"He is sincere," the Abbess said with a note of wonder in her voice. "It is almost like a miracle."

"Of course I am sincere," Hisoku cried. "Do you not think I am capable of overcoming you both if I wanted to? But I am held back by my reluctance to commit murder in this holy place, as well as by my admiration for you."

"It is a miracle," Tama said. "I need someone I can

send to Matsutani to collect some essential documents. If you can do this for me, and if I regain my estate as a result, I will let you serve me."

"Then tell me what you need," Hisoku said, "and I will leave tomorrow as soon as it is light."

14

KIYOYORI

Kiyoyori had been confined to Matsutani all winter by heavy snowfalls, cut off from any news of the Emperor's health or the fate of his son, Tsumaru. He heard neither from the steward Taro nor from Ryusonji. He tried to curb his impatience and anxiety by making meticulous preparations for the spring, which he was sure would bring some revolt or uprising, if not outright war. He did not speak to Tama, though he knew he could not put off a decision about her future for much longer. He could not forgive her for her actions at the beginning of the winter. As soon as the snows melted he sent men deep into the Darkwood, searching for any trace of Sesshin and Shikanoko, and, he hoped secretly, of Lady Tora.

One day Tsuneto returned with the news that the fugitives had been captured at Kumayama and handed over to the monk Gessho.

"They have been in Ryusonji all winter, then," Kiyoyori said. "Why have I heard nothing?"

"If they are not dead, they will be prisoners," Tsuneto replied.

"Did you speak to Sademasa at Kumayama?"

"I did."

"You know Shikanoko claimed to be his nephew, the son of Shigetomo, the former lord of Kumayama? Did he have anything to say about that?"

"Sademasa referred to him as an imposter," Tsuneto said. "I gather he was more than happy to have him removed so conveniently. He is not expecting him to return to make any further claims."

"So, the Prince Abbot has obtained what he sought from me—Master Sesshin. Why has he not returned my son?"

"Presumably he hopes to influence you in other matters," Tsuneto said.

Or he no longer has him, Kiyoyori thought. *Taro succeeded in rescuing him. But where are they?* He heard over and over in his mind the child's farewell cries: *Father! Don't go!* He remembered with startling clarity the evening after Akuzenji's attack when the bandits were executed and his wife had brought the children to eat with him. He had played with them and admired them, and then he had left and gone to Lady Tora and become enmeshed with her. Was that what had brought the punishment of Heaven down on him? Yet he would face ten times that punishment to be with her again. His grief welled up and

145

threatened to overcome him. He forced himself to listen to Tsuneto's words.

"Sademasa was very closemouthed about his own activities, but I noticed he has also spent the winter preparing for war. And he had several warriors with him whom I did not recognize. I wondered if they might have joined him from the east."

"He is planning to betray us?"

"He is an opportunist. He hinted he expects great rewards from the Prince Abbot for handing over Sesshin and Shikanoko. If you and the Crown Prince prevail he will cleave to you, but if the Prince's defeat seems imminent he will join the Miboshi."

"I need him to be staunch now more than ever. I must go to the capital myself as soon as possible and I don't like to leave Matsutani unguarded in these dangerous times."

These and other worries meant that Kiyoyori hardly slept that night, and so he was awake when the earthquake struck, and was able to escape with Hina. Much of the main building collapsed and the stables were destroyed in the fire that followed. The stonework of the lake was broken in several places and the lake drained away, leaving a muddy floor in which, when he got around to looking at it, Tama's footprints were clearly visible. He lost twenty horses, including his favorite black stallion, and ten people died. He entrusted Hina to Haru, hoping she would be comforted by playing with the children, but later that day when he went to assess the damage to the west gate he found her there, poking through the rubble. The gateposts still stood erect, but the roof and the transom had fallen to the ground.

"What are you doing there?"

Lost in some world of her own, she was startled by his voice. He was shocked by her pale face and noticed for the first time how thin she had become. The earthquake was the most recent in a series of shocks for her—Tsumaru's disappearance, the blinding of Sesshin, her stepmother's imprisonment. He felt guilty that he had not been more considerate toward her all winter. He had left her to Haru's care. Now he spoke more gently.

"Stay away from the gate; the beams might fall on you."

"I am looking for the eyes, Father. I had a dream I found them and put them in a treasure box. The gateposts were shaking with laughter. It was horrible. When I woke up the earth was shaking."

He noticed she had been crying. He saw a slight gleam in the dust and bent to lift the carved transom that had been half-buried in rubble. The eyes stared back at him. They had lost none of their luster.

"Ah," Hina said. Two tears fell on the eyes, moistening them. She held out a carved wooden box in which she had placed a small piece of white cloth. "Put them in here and I will keep them safe."

He took the cloth and picked up the eyes with it, wrapped them, and placed them in the box. She held the box awkwardly because she also had a sheaf of manuscripts, loosely bound with thread, clamped under one arm.

Kiyoyori gestured at the text. "Give me that, you are going to drop it."

She turned sideways so he could take it. It was a manuscript made up of folded pages, some yellow with black writing, some indigo with gold. He fanned through the pages, noting how some seemed to be glued together so he could not open them, while others were so blurred they were impossible to read. Occasionally a drawing of an animal or a mythical creature appeared, and he had the uneasy feeling their eyes were looking back at him. It resembled an esoteric text, the sort written by monks or healers.

"It's about medicine. Is it one of Master Sesshin's?"

"He gave it to me last year, after he saw me making potions for that dog that was so sick."

This surprised Kiyoyori. He had not known Sesshin had ever spoken to Hina, let alone given her a text like this. "Can you read it?"

"It's too difficult for me. But I like looking at the pictures. It's called the Kudzu Vine Treasure Store. That's because it's difficult and complicated like kudzu. Master Sesshin told me that. Sometimes I feel it doesn't want me to read it."

"I will help you if you are really interested." He made the promise knowing it was possible he would never keep it, that they would never have that sort of time together in the future, and again he deeply regretted squandering the time they might have had during the winter.

She nodded with a smile, but then her face turned grave. "Where is my stepmother?"

"I don't know. She walked away, probably early this morning."

He went with Hina to the lake and showed her the footprints. Hina stared at them. "Will she come back?"

"I don't think so."

"Will Tsumaru?"

"I am going to tell you a secret about Tsumaru," Kiyoyori said slowly. "You know he was kidnapped to make me hand over Master Sesshin . . ."

His daughter fixed him with a gaze like steel. "And Lady Tora?"

"I don't want to talk about Lady Tora with you; it is not fitting. When you are older you will understand."

Hina flushed at the rebuke. Kiyoyori went on sternly, trying to mask his guilt and regret. "Someone, one of our people, promised to rescue him. I don't know if he succeeded or not."

"Who?" she said flatly.

"A servant in the house below Rokujo. Iida no Taro is his name."

"If he did succeed, why has Tsumaru not come home?"

"I don't know," Kiyoyori replied. "But that is why I have to go to the capital, to find out."

"You won't leave me here?"

"No, you can come with me."

Hina said, "Was the earthquake a punishment?"

He did not want to answer her. It was not right for children to judge their parents. But he feared that the earthquake was a punishment for the many terrible things that had happened at Matsutani, and it was certainly an ominous start to the year.

They camped in the undamaged part of the house while the funerals were held and the bodies burned and while Kiyoyori issued instructions for the rebuilding. He left two thirds of his men to help with the work and guard Matsutani, and took the remainder with him to Miyako.

Hina took the text called the Kudzu Vine Treasure Store and the box containing Sesshin's eyes.

※

The city was tense, many armed warriors thronging the streets, the red banners of the Kakizuki flying from gates and roofs. As he passed through the southern gate, where beggars and other vagrants sought shelter, he was recognized in the middle of the chaos by one of Lord Masafusa's retainers, who was in charge of the guards.

The man greeted him warmly. "Kiyoyori! You have come to defend the capital?"

"What is happening?" Kiyoyori shouted back.

The other fought his way through the crowd, grasped the horse's bridle, and gestured to Kiyoyori to bend down. He whispered, "The Emperor is finally dying, and the Miboshi are approaching from the east."

"I would be more use at Matsutani, defending the high road," he said, wondering if he should turn back. He felt every decision he made was the wrong one, as though whatever divine protection he had been under had been withdrawn.

"No, you are needed here. We fear an attack on the Crown Prince. How many men have you brought?"

"Barely fifty. You did not hear about the earthquake?"

"We felt it here, but it was not destructive. You had better report to Lord Masafusa as soon as you can, and he will tell you what to do."

Kiyoyori acquiesced and rode on.

There was no sign of Taro at his house below Rokujo and the place looked even more neglected than before. He unleashed his anxiety on the servants in a blast of rage that had them scurrying around, opening shutters, airing the bedding, sweeping floors, and preparing food.

Hina was white with exhaustion. He himself bathed her face and feet and as soon as a room was ready made her lie down. Then he found paper and writing materials and sent Sadaike with a message to Ryusonji.

The man came back within the hour. The Prince Abbot would receive him even though it was getting late. Kiyoyori left at once, taking the ox carriage he reserved for travel within the capital, especially when he did not wish his face to be seen. The carriage was full of spiders and smelled of mold; the ox had not been in harness for months and had forgotten all its training. Other carriages packed the streets as the city's inhabitants prepared for flight. It took a long time to get to the temple, and when he arrived it was already twilight. The sky was clear and stars were appearing.

The carriage was not allowed beyond the first gate. Kiyoyori descended and was led across the gravel and through the temple buildings to the same reception room he had been in last time. The Prince Abbot sat on the same purple and white silk cushions. At his side knelt a young man whose head was not shaved and whose hair was tied up like a warrior's. He raised his head when Kiyoyori came in, and Kiyoyori recognized Shikanoko.

His instinctive response was relief that the boy was alive, but this was quickly replaced by rage. Shika did not look like a prisoner or a hostage. He must have allied himself with the Prince Abbot. How deeply Kiyoyori regretted sparing his life. But he could not waste time dwelling on that now. He knelt, waited for permission to speak, and then said, striving for politeness, "My lord Abbot, I heard that your monk Gessho was successful in tracking down the fugitives you sought. I see you have Shikanoko at your side, apparently in your service. So why has my son not been restored?"

The Prince Abbot answered him coldly. "There are still outstanding matters that need to be settled between us. Where is the woman, the sorceress? And where is your allegiance now? Whose side will you take?"

For a moment he could not speak. *He thinks she is alive!* Then he said, letting his anger show, "Who can I side with but my family, the Kakizuki? It is less than noble of you to expect me to betray my allegiance for my son's life."

The Prince Abbot's voice took on a note of fury. "You dare lecture me on nobility?" He half-rose as if he would step toward Kiyoyori, even strike him, but then he gained control and sat again. He tapped a scroll that lay on its own cushion at his side. "Do you know what this is? It is the Book of the Future. In it are inscribed the names of all the emperors to come, down through the ages. I am not acting idly or through the desire for personal gain. I am following the will of Heaven. Prince Momozono's name is not in it. But his younger brother's is."

"Show me," Kiyoyori demanded.

"Only my eyes can read it," the Prince Abbot replied.

How very convenient! Kiyoyori was assessing rapidly the attempted distraction, the apparent loss of control. He said boldly, "Show my son to me, Your Holiness. Just let me see his face."

"Agree not to oppose me, to stay out of the coming confrontation, and you may see him."

There was a note of uncertainty in his voice. Kiyoyori realized the Prince Abbot did not have Tsumaru. Had Taro been successful? He glanced at Shikanoko and saw that the young man was regarding him with pity. A jolt of fear struck him in the belly.

"Why do you waste my time?" the Prince Abbot said angrily. "I regret even agreeing to see you. Go. We have nothing more to discuss, now or ever again. The next time I see your face your head will be on a stake, along with all my enemies."

Kiyoyori left, half-expecting to be detained before he reached the gates and even more disturbed than he had been when he arrived. As he crossed the last courtyard, he heard the sounds of a lute and a voice singing:

The dragon child, he flew too high
He was still so young, he tried his best.

But his wings failed and he fell to earth.
He fell to earth.
Now he dwells beneath the lake at Ryusonji.

The plaintive tune sent a shiver down his spine.

He returned home, left the carriage, and rode on horseback to his kinsman Hosokawa no Masafusa's palace. Armed men gathered in the courtyard, swords at their hips, quivers filled with arrows on their backs, bows in their hands. Night had fallen.

Masafusa greeted him tensely. "You are here, Kiyo-yori? I was afraid you would have been already defeated by the Miboshi. Is anyone defending your estates?"

"I left most of my men there, about a hundred. The place was badly damaged in the earthquake. We had several dead and lost many horses. I had no idea the situation had become so desperate so quickly. Why was I not told?"

"We didn't realize the extent of the Prince Abbot's intrigues or the Miboshi's war preparations. While the Emperor lived, there was no cause for alarm. He had always designated Prince Momozono as his heir. But now he is dying—indeed, come close, let me whisper: it is rumored he already passed away some days ago, but the Prince Abbot will not allow it to be revealed until the Crown Prince and his son, Yoshimori, are dead, and he can immediately place his favorite on the Lotus Throne."

"Surely even he will not dare to harm His Imperial Highness?"

"Make no mistake, he will dare. He will accuse the

Prince of rebellion and attack his palace—it could be at any time, maybe even tonight. The Miboshi are approaching from the east, ready to take the capital and defend the claim of the new emperor."

"Where is our lord and what are his commands?" Kiyoyori said.

"He believes we should flee. The years of power and excess it seems have sapped his fighting spirit. Our men have little taste for war. Maybe our time has come to yield to the Miboshi."

"Not while I live!" Kiyoyori replied. He was glad the time for fighting had come. Nothing else would assuage his unease.

"I knew I could count on you. Lord Keita wants to take his grandson with him. That way he will protect the rightful emperor even if Prince Momozono should not survive. Go to the Prince's palace, defend it as long as you can, but most important, rescue the boy and bring him to Rakuhara, where our lord will take refuge."

Rakuhara was a large Kakizuki estate to the west of the capital near the port of Akashi.

"Go at once," Masafusa said.

Kiyoyori bowed his head. "I will see you in Rakuhara."

He reflected grimly as he hastened back through the dark street on how children were used as pawns in men's struggles for power. His son, Tsumaru, the Emperor's grandson, Yoshimori, were to be abducted, hidden, murdered, not for any crime of theirs, unless it was from a former life, but because of who their fathers were.

The lute player's song came into his head. Why had he heard it at that moment and what message did it have for him? But in his heart he knew its meaning was that Tsumaru was already dead.

✳

Hina had fallen asleep almost immediately after her father left and had slept deeply for a while, but the sound of men and horses awakened her. She was afraid her father was going somewhere and leaving her behind, and she ran out onto the veranda, but he had already gone.

It was a still spring night. The scent of blossom floated over the neglected garden and now and then a fish splashed in the pond.

Something moved in the shadows. She thought it might be a fox and pressed closer to a veranda pillar. The figure approached, walking on two legs. She was about to scream when she saw it was Shikanoko.

He put his finger to his lips and beckoned to her to come closer, then put his hand on her shoulder and took her to the end of the garden. Azalea bushes had grown wild and she could see their blossoms faintly. She was happy to see Shika. She had missed him since he and Sesshin had been driven away.

"Hina," he whispered, "where is your father?"

"He has gone out. I don't know where."

"He came to Ryusonji," Shika said. "I saw him there. But hasn't he returned?"

"I was asleep," she replied. "He must have come back

and left again, for I thought I heard him depart with men and horses."

"I wanted to speak to him, to try to explain things to him—but now it is too late." Shika was silent for a few moments. "Well, I suppose I must tell you, though it is a hard thing for a child to hear."

"Is it about Tsumaru? Is he dead?" She was shivering. Shika put his arm around her.

"How did you know?"

"I dream about him and he is always a spirit in my dreams."

Shika sighed and said, "You must tell your father how it happened. Tsumaru disappeared from Ryusonji, the first night I was there. The Prince Abbot was distraught. He had grown very fond of him, and he had promised your father no harm would come to him. He performed a spirit-return ritual and learned that someone in your father's service had tried to snatch him away. While keeping him silent he had suffocated him by mistake. We found his body in the lake."

Hina was crying silently. Shika said, "He is with the dragon child now."

"Father told me who it was." Hina wept. "He was going to rescue Tsumaru, and he killed him. It was Iida no Taro."

"I will remember that name," Shika said.

She leaned against him. "I missed you. And the horses. How is Risu?"

"She is improving in temper. She is in love with Nyorin. I think she will have a foal next year."

"I wish I could see it. I wish I could live with you and Risu and Nyorin and their foal. Why don't we get married when I am old enough?"

"Your father will want you to marry a great lord, someone of your high station."

"I would rather marry you."

There came a distant sound of shouting, the whine of humming arrows, the clash of steel, then screams of horses and men.

"What's happening?" Hina's fingers ground into Shika's arm.

"It has started," he replied. "I must go back to Ryusonji."

"Shikanoko, are you on our side or someone else's?"

"I am on no one's side. Only my own."

"So you are a sorcerer like everyone says?"

"I was made one against my will, and now it is my fate, it seems."

"You sound so sad about it."

"I wanted to talk to your father. I am sad that it is too late. If you see him tell him I am sorry . . ."

"Sorry for what?"

"I don't know, sorry he spared my life that day."

"I'm not sorry! I'm glad. I thought he would kill you like all the others. I prayed and prayed that your life would be spared. And I was so happy when you took Risu as well as Nyorin. I was afraid you were going to abandon her. I liked you as soon as I saw you, but I really liked you after that."

"Hina!" he exclaimed. "What a gentle child you are!" Then he drew her closer and looked at her face intently.

"What is it?" she whispered.

"I want to remember how you look. We may never meet again."

Neither of them spoke for a moment. Then Hina said, "I have Master Sesshin's eyes. Shall I give them to you?"

"Why did you take them from the gate?"

"There was an earthquake," she said in exasperation. "Didn't you know? The house was destroyed and the stables. Lots of horses were killed and some people, too. And my stepmother ran away."

She was crying again.

"He intended his eyes to remain at Matsutani," Shika said. "But now you must keep them with you. Wash them with your tears and they will watch over you." He held her for a moment, then released her, leaped over the wall in one bound, and was gone.

Hina returned to the house. The clamor from the streets had awakened the maids. They clustered around her in fear. She sat on the veranda with the box containing the eyes and the Kudzu Vine Treasure Store, waiting for her father. From time to time she allowed tears to fall in order to moisten the eyes, but she could not tell if they were watching over her or what protection they could give her.

15

AKI

Aki woke from a vivid dream—she was standing by a stream, she saw splashes of blood on the rocks, then a young stag leaped toward her. She opened her eyes. Lamps burned feebly in each corner of the room, but outside it was dark and still. No birds sang yet, not even the cocks were crowing.

Her father was kneeling beside her, wearing a hunting robe, beneath which she glimpsed green-laced armor. His long sword was at his hip. Her mother stood behind him, holding his quiver of arrows.

"They are coming to arrest the Prince," her father said quietly.

Aki's heart was racing. She breathed slowly and deliberately in the way he had taught her, her gaze fixed on his. She wanted to relate the dream to him and hear his opinion of it, what it meant, whether it was auspicious, but there was no time now.

"He will not be captured," her father went on. "He will not let them execute him in secret so they can put their puppet on the Lotus Throne. We have sent for help. Kiyoyori is coming. We will defend ourselves for as long as possible. You must take His Highness and escape."

He turned and took the quiver from his wife and fastened it to his back. "Wake him up quickly and dress him in some old clothes."

Aki's mother said, "Better they should both cross the river of death here with us. How will a girl survive on her own? Where will she go?"

"We must give Yoshimori a chance," her father replied.

"I'll take him. I'll look after him. I promise." She was on her feet now. "What shall I wear? Do you have something old for me?"

Her mother brought a pile of maid's clothes. "Even these are too fine," she grumbled. "Look at her, nothing can hide her appearance. There are bad men out there. What will they do to her?"

"This is why I have taught her to defend herself," her father said. "Take your knife, Aki, and promise you will stay away from men—you know what I am talking about. There are dangers women face that men do not. Kill anyone who tries to get intimate with you or who tries to hurt the Prince."

"I promise," she said.

"I will cut her hair," her mother said, and called for a maid to bring scissors. Aki's hair reached almost to the ground. Her mother held each strand close to her head and snipped through it, allowing them to fall around her until she seemed to be standing in a pool of black. Neither of them spoke or wept.

When it was done and Aki had finished dressing, her mother brought Yoshimori and changed his embroidered sleeping robe for one of rough hemp, tied with a rope cord. His eyes were heavy with sleep and he yawned deeply, but he did not cry out or protest.

Aki's head felt light and cold. She wrapped a cowl around it, as though she were a town girl going early to market or visiting a shrine. She had never met or talked to a town girl in her life; it seemed an exotic thing to pretend to be.

"Where shall I go?"

"Follow the north road around the lake and head for the temple, Rinrakuji. You remember we have often been there together. The monks will hide the young Prince there and you can be what you were dedicated to be, a shrine maiden in the service of Kannon. Stay with him until he is safe. You must take your catalpa bow, we have wrapped it with Genzo, the imperial lute—we cannot let that be destroyed."

Her mother handed the bundle to her. She took it with reverent hands, and felt the lute vibrate through the carrying cloth. It gave a single soft, grief-filled twang, and the bow responded.

"Go now, my daughter," her father said. "The Prince Abbot's men will be here at any moment. We will hold them off at the main gate. You must slip through the Moon Gate at the rear and follow the river. There will be many people fleeing the city. Mingle with them."

He knelt before the boy. "Yoshimori, you must not be

called Prince or Lord for a while. No one must know who you are. Do not speak to anyone. Obey Aki in everything. She is your older sister now. Do you understand?"

"What about Kai?" Yoshi said. "I'm not going anywhere without Kai."

"It is hard enough with one child, let alone two," Aki's father murmured.

"If Kai stays she will die," her mother said, just loud enough for Yoshimori to hear her.

"I'll scream," he said. "If Kai doesn't come I'll scream and scream. And I won't go anywhere."

"Wake her up," Aki said. "I can take them both. Kai will make things easier."

Tears sprang from her father's eyes. Her mother was weeping silently as she thrust two pairs of clogs into Aki's hands. Aki bowed to the ground before her parents. She did not speak, but in her heart she was crying, *Father, Mother, when will I see you again?*

Noise was erupting like a rainstorm: first the spattering drops, a single cry, the urgent thud of feet hurrying along a corridor, then the heavier fall, women wailing, the tread of men running, shouts, in the distance the shrill neighing of horses. Aki lifted Yoshimori in her arms and settled him on her hip. He was a slight child and she was strong, unlike most palace women, who never lifted anything heavier than a writing brush or a hair comb; even so, she did not know how far she would be able to carry him.

Kai appeared at her side, pale and silent. She was holding Aki's ritual box.

"Your mother told me to bring this," she said.

"I can't carry it, too!" Aki exclaimed, near tears for the first time.

"I'll look after it," Kai said. She touched Yoshimori on the ankle and smiled up at him.

Lights flickered, throwing strange shadows on the brocade-and-bamboo blinds that covered the entrances to the rooms. Aki pushed the closest blind aside and stepped out onto the wide veranda. She set Yoshimori down on the edge and put on her clogs, fitting the other pair to his feet. Taking him by the hand, she pulled him upright.

"Now you must walk beside me."

For a moment she thought she would have to show him how, but, though he had been carried almost everywhere throughout his short life, his muscles were not yet useless and he was still young enough to want to walk, even to run, like any normal child. Kai followed barefoot. They went swiftly across the darkness of the Eastern Courtyard, but as they passed the New Shining Hall a sudden light flared, revealing the face of Yoshimori's mother, known as Lady Shinmei'in.

Aki pulled the cowl lower over her face and tried to hide the boy in the skirt of her robe. For a moment she thought they would pass by unrecognized, but the Princess leaned toward them.

"What are you doing with His Highness? Where are you taking him?"

"I must not be called that," the boy said.

"Lady, I am his nurse's daughter. My father, Hidetake, told me to escape with your son, into hiding."

"Why? What is happening?"

"The Prince Abbot has sent men to arrest your husband. The Prince intends to resist."

Lady Shinmei'in's eyes were huge, her face as pale as snow. "Then I must be at his side and share his pillow in death as in life. Our son must die with us. Come, Your Highness. We will change these base garments and prepare your illustrious body for the next world." She held out her arms, slender and white against the black hair that fell like silk around her. "No one can escape his fate."

The boy hardly knew his mother. He had been brought up by Aki's parents. He shrank closer to Aki's side and gripped Kai's hand.

What was Aki to do? Should she obey her father and defy the Princess? Or should she recognize the mother's right to decide the fate of her child, relinquish him, and return to die alongside her own parents? What was there to fear in death? It lay all around, separated from life by only the thinnest of membranes. A moment's exhilarating pain and then you passed through to the other world, leaving behind honor and courage as your memorial, facing judgment and then rebirth.

In the dim light the mother's pale hands beckoned like a ghost's toward the grave. The child said, "If I am to reign I cannot die now."

Until they are seven, children belong to the gods and speak only truth. Aki knew she was hearing a divine message. Without saying anything she seized Yoshimori's hand. For a moment he resisted in surprise, but then he surrendered to her grip and the three of them were running toward the Moon Gate and the river.

There were many people trying to escape, for the attackers, the Prince Abbot's men, were setting the palace buildings on fire, one after another. The wind that sprang up just before dawn was driving the flames westward toward the city. Already the Hall of Light from the East was alight, and next to it the Hall of New Learning stood gutted, its rafters black against the red inferno. Priceless treasures, irreplaceable scrolls were being consumed and reduced to ashes. She felt the lute in her hand vibrate again and moan softly.

Yoshimori was quivering, too, tremors running from his hand to hers. She bent and whispered, "Be brave. Remember your own words. Your destiny is to live."

He made no reply, but his grip tightened and as they hurried through the gate, rather than she being the guide, he was leading her.

Kai stopped for a moment and made a sign to Aki.

From behind Aki heard a great shout, as if one of the gods had appeared and was announcing his presence.

"I am Kiyoyori of the Kakizuki, lord of Matsutani and Kuromori."

The girls looked at each other with wide, startled eyes and then hurried Yoshi on toward the river.

KIYOYORI

Kiyoyori had ridden straight from Masafusa's residence to the Crown Prince's palace. It was not far away, on the east side of the Greater Palace compound where the Emperor lived (and presumably now lay dead). As he and his small band of men forced their way through the streets, he thought of Hina left alone, wondered if he would ever see her again, if anyone would stay and look after her or if they would all run away, wondered what had happened to his steward, Iida no Taro, and then saw the man himself, standing on the corner of an alley.

Taro's face changed at the sight of Kiyoyori. It was as if he had been waiting for him. For a moment hope shot through him. *He brings good news. Tsumaru is alive, hidden somewhere in safety.* But then Taro made a helpless gesture and Kiyoyori understood.

I must talk to him. I must find out what happened. He

was prepared to face death, but he could not bear the thought of not knowing the manner in which his son had passed over before him.

There was no time. The horses swept past. Kiyoyori turned in the saddle briefly and saw Taro begin to run after him, weaving through the crowd. His horse shied, and he looked ahead again.

It was around the end of the hour of the ox, still a while before dawn. The gates of the palace were barred with armed men on both sides. He could see at a glance they were too few. He stationed his men on the outside facing the street, and then convinced the guards he was who he claimed to be and that they should summon someone to speak to him. A nobleman came out, leading his horse, and the guards closed the gate behind him.

Kiyoyori knew him slightly—Lord Hidetake.

"Kiyoyori," Hidetake said in relief. "You have arrived just in time. We received word an hour ago that an attack is imminent. The Prince is putting on his armor now."

"I would stay and fight alongside you," Kiyoyori said, leaning down from his horse. "But Lord Keita has ordered me to rescue his grandson and escort him to Rakuhara."

"So, Keita is fleeing," Hidetake said. "He will not come to our aid?"

"At least we can save Yoshimori if we act quickly. Where is he?"

"I have already sent him away. My daughter is taking him to Rinrakuji."

"I must go after them," Kiyoyori said, but at that moment the sound of horses coming up the street made them both turn. Men carried torches that showed their weapons and their helmets. They stopped just beyond arrow's reach and their leader announced, "I am Yoshibara no Chikataka of the Miboshi. I have been sent by Lord Aritomo and His Holiness the Prince Abbot of Ryusonji to arrest Prince Momozono for inciting rebellion against the Emperor."

Kiyoyori rode toward them, announcing his name in a voice louder than thunder.

"We serve his Imperial Highness and we will never surrender him to you."

"You should have stayed in Kuromori, Kiyoyori. The Shimaura barrier has fallen and fifty thousand Miboshi are advancing on the capital."

"Then we will die here and you with us," Kiyoyori replied, grim elation welling up in him, sharpening his vision and strengthening his arm.

The gates behind him opened and the Crown Prince himself rode out, at the head of a hundred men. As they swept past Kiyoyori, Hidetake leaped onto his horse, took up his bow, and set an arrow to it. The horsemen all had bows ready and a hail of arrows sped toward the Miboshi, making them fall back momentarily. Kiyoyori thought the Prince had the numbers and the will to prevail, but hundreds more men had been waiting out of sight in the alleys. Now, with white banners gleaming in the light of torches, they rushed into the broad avenue, letting fly a barrage of arrows. Prince Momozono was hit in the throat. Kiyoyori galloped toward him, but his own horse screamed and staggered, its chest pierced. He jumped from it as it fell.

A circle had formed around the wounded Crown Prince as his men strove to defend him, fighting hand to hand with swords, pikes, and daggers. One by one they fell, their lifeblood mingling with that of their prince. Kiyoyori saw there was no hope; they were completely overwhelmed by the mass of the Miboshi. His own men formed a larger semicircle, their backs to the gate. Kiyoyori remembered his orders to rescue the child, now almost certainly the Emperor. He did not want to be thought to be fleeing, but he had to save the child. Shouting to his men to fall back behind him and protect the entrance, he ran inside the gate, closing it himself. His last sight of the battle was Sadaike, blood streaming from a head wound, gesturing to show he understood.

The palace was already on fire—attackers must have broken through the other gates, unless there were traitors inside the Prince's household—and women ran shrieking from the flames. Kiyoyori ran, too, hoping to catch up with Hidetake's daughter before she left the compound. He was brought to a halt by the sight of Lord Keita's daughter, Lady Shinmei'in, the child's mother, standing outlined against the blackened pillars and rafters of what had once been a great hall.

"Lady," he called, "where is your son? I am sent to find him and you. Your father commanded me to come. I am Kakizuki."

She held a dagger in her hand. Her eyes gazed on him without seeing him.

"My son, I come to join you," she said, so softly he could hardly hear her against the roar of the flames and the crash of falling beams.

She slashed her throat with the blade. Blood flew, covering him. She stood for a long moment, her eyes huge, her hands fluttering. Then she crumpled before him.

Miboshi men burst into the courtyard. Kiyoyori turned to face them, his long sword in his hand. He had no fear, just a resolve to take as many as possible into death with him and on to Hell afterward. The sight of him, covered in blood, surrounded by flames, made them pause for a moment, and in that sliver of time a man appeared at his side like a shadow. Taro.

"What are you doing here?" he shouted.

"I have to tell you about Tsumaru!"

"What is there to tell? That he is dead and you killed him?"

"The dragon child took him. It's true he died, in the lake, but he lives on in the dragon child."

A Miboshi warrior ran screaming toward them. Kiyoyori felled him with one sweep of his sword.

"It was my fault," Taro cried over the clamor. "I am going to die with you and when we face the Judge of Hell I will take your place."

"If we don't both die here I will pursue you and kill you," Kiyoyori yelled, ducking to avoid a sword thrust, then parrying the returning stroke, disarming the blade's owner and skewering him. He wrenched at his sword to release it and slipped in the pool of blood. Taro stepped in front of him to protect him while he recovered his footing.

"I could not be a warrior in life," he said, bending over Kiyoyori. "Maybe I will be one in death."

17

AKI

Aki's father had trained her in the arts of war. She had practiced for many hours on the polished floors of the halls of Rinrakuji, she had ridden horses and shot arrows at their country estate, Nishimi, on the shores of Lake Kasumi, but she had never been out in the city on her own or mingled with common people. She did not know how to beg, or steal, or barter for food. Yoshimori had hardly ever walked on his own two feet in the palace, let alone outside in the dark over a rutted road filled with people, oxen, carts, horses, all flooding toward the northern gates of the city, and the river.

The temple, Rinrakuji, where her father had told her to seek refuge, was on the eastern side of the lake, a long way to the north. As her father had said, she had been there many times before, but she had only rarely gone there by road, more often by boat from Nishimi. It took a couple of hours across the lake, no more, but now she had to make her way from the south, either by road or over water from Kasumiguchi, where the two roads from the north converged at the barrier.

Cocks were crowing and in the east the sky was turning pale. Behind them the city burned like another fiery dawn in the south. Yoshimori's eyes were wide with shock and disgust at the smell, the rude jostling, the unpleasant closeness of so many bodies, but he did not cry out or complain, just clutched Kai's hand as if he would never let it go. Kai said nothing, her small face set in an expression of determination. Aki's mother had tied a scarf around her head, but it could not completely hide the long hair. She was limping a little.

Aki caught snatches of information: the barrier towns to the east had fallen, the Miboshi were pouring into the city from the south, the Kakizuki were fleeing . . .

Many in the crowd wavered, some deciding to follow the Kakizuki and taking the road to the west, some pressing on to Kasumiguchi. Aki reasoned the town would be in enough confusion to allow them to slip through the barrier. Maybe they could take a boat there; if not, they would follow the road along the east side of the lake.

The boy was getting tired. He leaned against her, his feet dragged. The lute was heavy; she changed arms and felt its muted response to the movement. As the light grew she could see the river on their right. Horses and men towed boats upstream; none were returning to Miyako. Some of them carried produce, lumber, casks of rice wine and vinegar, barrels of grain. One boat was laden with musicians and young women dressed in robes of scarlet silk, holding parasols decorated with moons. The musicians played, lute, flute, harp, and drum, and the women sang, their voices ringing out in the cool dawn air.

Kai was staring at them. "What beautiful ladies," she said.

Yoshi waved to them. "I wish we could ride in the boat with them!"

His refined speech caught the attention of a man walking beside them. "Beautiful ladies!" he scoffed. "You're a bit young for a ride with them! But you're a pretty boy— get on that boat and someone will ride you. And those pretty girls, too."

He thrust his pockmarked face toward them, leering. Aki's hand was on her dagger as she pulled Yoshi away.

"You must not speak," she whispered. "Didn't my father make that clear?"

A few paces later they came upon a dead body. A man lay on his back, grinning vacantly at the sky, blood congealing around the wound in his throat where flies crawled. Who could he have been? Aki wondered. Victim of a robbery, perhaps, or the thief himself, dealt a rough justice. Or maybe just some unfortunate who had offended the wrong person. She wished she had not just mentioned her father, for now she could not stop thinking about him, and her mother, and them both dead.

Yoshi went white, swayed on his feet, and vomited a rush of yellow liquid. Aki knelt beside him, wiped his face and mouth. He was crying silently. Kai was also in tears.

The same pockmarked man came close, saying, "Here,

I'll carry the little lord for a while," but Aki saw something lascivious in his face and drew out the dagger, backing away, her arm around Yoshi.

"Oh, an armed girl, a young warrior!" The man's leer embraced her, too. "Never been opened by a man, I'll wager. I'll take you first and then the boy, and sell the little girl."

They were at the water's edge. She could back away no farther. A horse came between them and the man, its handler shouting at them to get out of the way before the two ropes fastened to the bow and the stern threw them into the water beneath the boat's hull.

A woman's voice called to her from the deck. "Give us the children, little sister, and then jump yourself." Aki just had time to realize it was another pleasure boat, filled with musicians, when many hands reached out and seemed to pluck Yoshi, and then Kai, from her. She tucked the dagger in her belt, a woman took her hand, and she leaped onto the boat, clutching the bundle with the other, terrified the lute would fall into the water. It moaned with its almost-human voice.

On the shore the man made a vulgar gesture toward her and yelled something she did not understand.

"Don't worry about him," the woman said, the same voice that had told her to jump. "Stay with us and you will come to no harm."

They had placed Yoshi on a bench covered with scarlet cloth and cushions embroidered with dragons and flowers. Kai stood beside him, still holding on to him, still clutching the ritual box. A young woman was bathing Yoshi's face and hands and another pressed a cup of lukewarm broth into Aki's hands.

"I did not even bring water with me," she said, horrified by her own helplessness. She had no idea how the world worked or who these people were. They had rescued her from one danger, but were they not simply another? How was she going to keep Yoshi safe? They were almost certainly alone in the world now, her parents dead, Yoshi's, too. Her eyes grew hot as she drank the broth, but she struggled not to let the tears fall.

"Where are you going, little sister?"

"I don't know exactly. Our parents are dead and we are fleeing from the fighting. Maybe we will go to Rinrakuji, maybe as far as Kitakami." Aki remembered the name of the port on the Northern Sea, even though she had never been there. "Where is this boat going?"

"To the fifteenth-day market at the Rainbow Bridge. We are entertainers. They call me Fuji."

She said it as though Aki should know her name, but it meant nothing to her nor had she ever heard of the market or the bridge. They sounded otherworldy and she wondered if she had been rescued by spirit beings or if she and the children had in fact fallen under the boat and drowned, and were now on one of the streams of the river of death.

Father, Mother, I will be with you soon!

There were several canopies on the boat covering soft-matted platforms, which could be made private behind bamboo blinds. Fuji led Aki onto one of these and the other women lifted Yoshi and laid him down beside her. His eyes closed, but he still gripped Kai's hand. She climbed awkwardly up next to him, putting the box close to his head. Fuji lowered the blind on the eastern side against the sun's rays. The shadows fell, striped and dappled, against their faces. Fuji leaned toward Aki and unwound the cowl that covered her head.

"What happened to your hair?" she exclaimed.

"My mother cut it."

"Did she intend you to be a nun? Is that why you are going to Rinrakuji?"

Aki nodded. "I am dedicated to the shrine of Kannon there."

"That explains the box." Fuji made a gesture toward it. "I thought it must be a ritual box."

"It's mine, Kai was just carrying it for me."

"How old are you?" Fuji said.

"Sixteen."

"And your brother?"

"He turned six this year."

Fuji narrowed her eyes. "From a different womb?"

"Yes, but the same father." Ten years was a long gap between siblings, two mothers was more plausible. So, had her mother died? Or been put aside for a younger woman? Suddenly there was a host of stories she might tell, but she had to remember what she said and to whom. And then her sister came into her mind, the child born the same day as Yoshi, who had died at birth, leaving her mother with milk for an infant prince.

"What about the little girl?" Fuji said. "Surely they are not twins?"

"No, the child of another woman. My stepmother took pity on her and raised her with her son."

"Come here, little one." Fuji reached out to Kai and tried to pull her toward her, but Yoshi tightened his grip.

Kai shook her head. "If I let go he'll scream. I always stay with him like this until he falls asleep."

Fuji stood and went closer. Kai shrank back as the woman took the scarf from her head. "What beautiful hair," she murmured, and then swept it back, revealing Kai's half-formed ears.

"Ah!" she cried in surprise. "That's too bad."

Kai stared back at her with her usual steady expression.

"What are we going to do with you?" Fuji said.

She sat down next to Aki, ran her hand over Aki's cropped head, and said nothing more for a few moments. Aki thought she looked disappointed. Fuji drew the dagger from Aki's belt and laid it down on the mat beside them, staring at it. Then she said, "What do you carry in the cloth? Is it an instrument?"

"Yes, a lute. And my catalpa bow."

"I can understand the bow, for it is part of your vocation, but the lute? It must be precious to you. You must play for us later."

"I am not at all skilled," she admitted.

"That's a pity, if it is true, for we need a lute player. Our last one was seduced away by a rich widow who fell in love with him and offered him a life of ease in Akashi."

She had been removing Aki's clothing while she spoke, until the girl sat in her underclothes, shivering a little.

Fuji studied her appraisingly. "It is a shame about your hair," she murmured. "You are well formed, even though your face lacks true beauty. Why don't you stay with us while it grows back, and then you can become one of us?"

"What would I have to do, apart from the music?" Aki said.

"We entertain men, soothe away their troubles, bring a smile to their faces, sing to them as their nurses or their mothers once did."

"I am already dedicated to the shrine," Aki said. "I must go to Rinrakuji. I should not *entertain men*."

"Nothing crude would be expected of you," Fuji said with a smile. "Your purity would not be compromised. Men come to us not in power but in supplication. They do not command, they entreat. Sex has a power of its own, which I know how to wield. This boat is my realm, my sisters and brothers are my subjects. Men visit us as ambassadors from a foreign country bringing tribute, seeking favors. But purity also has power. Your presence will strengthen us and bring us blessings. I already feel I love you like my own daughter. In return we will protect you and your little brother, and the other girl. Say you will at least come with us as far as Aomizu. It is only a day's walk to Rinrakuji from there. You can try life as a shrine maiden and if you don't like it you can come back to us."

"Thank you," Aki said, though she did not think there was any going back from the life that had been ordained for her. Fuji dressed her again with tender fingers like a mother's.

Aki lay down next to Yoshi and stroked his head. He was asleep now and stirred only very slightly at her touch. Kai had fallen asleep next to him. She listened to the noises of the boat, the musicians practicing, a woman singing. Then suddenly dream images began to form, the Princess, her father's face; they dissolved and she was asleep.

When she awoke the boat had come to a halt. Fuji was brushing her hair with her gentle fingers. Yoshi still slept beside her.

"Little sister, we need to get ready for our guests."

Aki looked around. She had no idea where she was, but the narrow river had widened into a vast lake, its surface as smooth and dark as steel. The boat, transformed with glowing red lanterns, was moored against a wooden pier that stretched out into the water. It was twilight and a thin gray mist rose from the lake, blurring the reflection of the lights and making the boat look as if it were suspended in the air. The musicians were warming up and the notes echoed in a random pattern that sounded enchanted.

"You will play with them?" Fuji said. It was only partly a question.

"Really, I have no skill," Aki said. She had thought the older woman kind before in the way she expected women to be, in the way, all her life, servants and waiting-women had been to her, but now she felt Fuji's strength and her dominance. No wonder she was the empress of her realm. Aki's flight had been driven by a mixture of excitement and desperation. Exhaustion had felled her. These emotions had given way to fear. She had entrusted Yoshi, Kai, and herself to these people—and what else could she have done?—but the enormity of what her father had asked of her began to sink in. The Emperor of the Eight Islands slept beside her. The sacred lute of the Lotus Throne lay on her other side. How was she going to keep them hidden, when the lute would reveal itself by its gold and pearl inlay, its rosewood frame?

Yet she could not refuse to unwrap it when Fuji told her to. Aki stared at the shabby old instrument, not recognizing it. It had changed its appearance completely. What could have happened? Did her father pick up the wrong instrument in the dark and confusion? Had someone stolen Genzo while she slept and replaced it with this ordinary, plain lute? Was the imperial treasure, preserved through the ages, lost through her fault, while in her hands? Then Yoshi would never be emperor and she had failed when she had hardly even begun.

She took it up with shaking hands, aware that Fuji was watching her intently. She knew how to hold the instrument, how to move her fingers over the strings, but she had no gift for music and, as a child and young girl, had always preferred her father's teaching and pursuits to her mother's. Now, using her nail as she had no plectrum, she began to pick out the notes to a children's song her mother used to sing. She made a face; even she could tell the lute was out of tune.

Yoshi awoke, rubbing his eyes. He began to sing in

his high childish voice. After a few lines Kai sat up and joined in.

Aki felt Genzo come alive. She felt its surprise, as though no one had actually played it for hundreds of years, and then its joy and delight as it found its tune and the notes began to pour from it.

"Astonishing," Fuji exclaimed. "Really, the three of you are quite enchanting."

Quickly they were dressed in red-and-white robes and placed among the musicians in the prow.

"Do you know this song?" the players asked, singing a few lines or picking out the notes, and Aki shook her head, only to feel Genzo vibrate beneath her fingers. There was no tune the lute did not know. So she played all night, watching the men—the guests, the ambassadors—come to visit the women and retire behind the bamboo blinds, to be entertained by them.

The moon rose and set, and it was almost dawn when the last guest departed. Gifts had been delivered in tribute: lengths of cloth, casks of rice, embroidery, sweet bean paste, fans, ceramic dishes. An early meal was prepared and then the women lay down and slept while the mooring ropes were cast off and the sail was raised. A single helmsman steered the boat along the coast toward the Rainbow Bridge.

Aki rewrapped Genzo in the carrying cloth and placed it next to Yoshi and Kai, bowing her head and thanking it. Before she slept she lifted a corner of the cloth to check it and saw the gleam of gold and pearl.

At one time, the island, Majima, had been part of the main-land, home to a lakeside village, but in the past fifty or so years the weather had changed, with long, heavy rains in summer and huge snowfalls in winter, so the water level in the lake had risen and several villages had been sub-merged. Now Majima was a three-cornered island, its rocky western point thrusting out into the lake, a pine-shaded beach on its eastern side. On its highest spot stood a shrine to Inari, the fox god, from which a row of vermilion gates led down to the curved wooden bridge, the Rainbow Bridge, that joined the island to the mainland.

Fuji told Aki that the local lord dreamed he should have a market at the end of the rainbow and the next day he saw one fall on Majima, so he had the bridge built.

"Why didn't he have the market on this side and save himself the trouble?" Aki said.

"Men love to build bridges," Fuji replied. "They love to join things together. The bridge is beautiful and sacred and, you know, markets are best held on islands, or riverbanks, places that are thresholds, removed from the everyday world. For there is a sort of magic going on at markets. Goods are bartered, one thing transformed into another. Craftsmen create something from nothing. Men trade the work of their hands and muscles. Everyone is equal, there are no mas-ters and servants, no lords and retainers."

Kai was listening intently. Yoshi shrank close to Aki and pulled her head down so he could whisper in her ear.

Fuji seemed to divine what he was saying. "You are afraid of pollution? What a little prince you are! Some would think your little friend a source of pollution with her shell ears. Where were you brought up? In the Imperial Palace? Let me guess, your father was a nobleman who either stayed to face the Miboshi and died in the capital or fled west with Lord Keita."

Aki did not know how to respond. Fuji pressed her. "Am I right?"

"Not really," Aki said, creating a story rapidly. "My parents were employed in a nobleman's palace. My mother cleaned and my father was a painter."

"A cleaner's daughter does not have such soft hands, a painter's son has sulfur and cinnabar under his nails!" Fuji laughed. "Don't worry. I won't tell anyone where you come from."

Aki felt the older woman believed she now knew a secret that gave her power over them and brought them under her control.

"We are considered a source of pollution, like many here at the market," Fuji said. "Wandering women who present puppet plays, men who build gardens and dig wells, changing the face of the earth, those who deal with death and decay, who bury corpses and demolish buildings, children who train animals and perform acrobatics. But don't you see, little lord, we, being their opposite, are closer to the divine and the sacred than is the everyday world where most people live. Your mother may have been a lady or a cleaner, but she still went to the threshold of death to bring you into the world, and the afterbirth that nourished you had to be buried, like everyone else's, in the gateway. You began life in blood and excrement and you will end it the same way. What you call pollution is not defilement; rather it is the essence of life, dangerous and dirty, maybe, but full of deep pleasure and power."

Yoshi gazed at her, not comprehending but impressed by her serious intensity.

"One day you will understand," Fuji said, and stroked his cheek with her slender fingers.

The blinds were lowered, the silk cushions spread out, and the women prepared to receive their guests. Aki again sat with the musicians with the lute. She made Yoshi sit next to her, Kai on the other side, and he sang with them; she could tell he was becoming bored, but she was afraid to let him out of her sight. When the musicians took a rest and Fuji was occupied behind the blinds, she let the children go to the side of the boat and they hung over the railing, gazing at everything going on around.

"Can we go ashore?" Yoshi said.

"I'd like to, but I don't know how to get there," Aki replied.

The boat was moored along with several others between the two shores. The visitors arrived in little vessels, hardly bigger than tubs, or were carried on the shoulders of porters, clambering on board with their feet wet and the hems of their robes soaked, making jokes about it that Aki blushed at, though she only half-understood them.

They asked for girls by name; they knew them well.

Their eyes were bright with anticipation and excitement. They aroused in Aki a curious mixture of interest and scorn.

"Look!" Yoshi said. "Monkeys! Children with monkeys!"

A strange troupe was making its way along the island shore. Not all of them were children, though they all wore children's clothes, in every shade of red, and all had the same wild, free look as though they were part child and part animal. They stopped opposite the boat and waved. Even the monkeys, tethered by long silken cords and braided collars, raised their little paws.

Yoshi waved back eagerly. One of the men started beating rhythmically on a small drum. A boy of about eight threw himself in the air, turning and tumbling. Two monkeys watched gravely and when he had finished imitated his routine in a bored, offhand way that the onlookers found most amusing. The boy became angry, the monkeys pretended to be scared and when he turned his back imitated his anger perfectly. The crowd roared with laughter.

A competition ensued, boy against monkeys, leaping ever higher, turning more and more somersaults. The monkeys won effortlessly.

The boy fell to the ground, discouraged and miserable. The monkeys looked anxious, conferred with each other, chattered pleadingly at the crowd as though seeking advice. They approached him silently and wrapped their arms around him. He leaped to his feet, grinning, while the monkeys clung around his neck and kissed his face.

"Oh!" Yoshi sighed. "I wish I were him!"

The acrobats were followed by a traveling physician

selling herbs, oils, and potions with long, complicated an-
ecdotes that made the crowd laugh, though Aki hardly
understood a word, and then an old man made his way
through the throng, stood on the shore, and waved to the
musicians.

They waved back excitedly and quickly arranged for
one of the porters to carry him over to the boat. When he
was on board, one of them dried his feet reverently with
a towel and the others gathered in a circle around him,
bowing their heads as he spoke a blessing.

Aki had never seen anyone like him, nor did she recognize the prayer. It was the time of the midday meal and
food was served, prepared by the market women, carried
across to the boat in baskets: rice with eggs stirred through
it, fresh fern heads and burdock root, grilled sweet fish
from the lake lying on young oak leaves, sweet bean paste
in many different flavors and forms.

The old man ate sparingly. At the end of the meal he
took the last of the rice and formed it into balls with his
fingers, spoke a blessing over them, and handed them
around. When Aki took one, his gaze fell on her, and on
Yoshi sitting on her lap.

"They are like the Lady and her Child," he said. "Call
on the name of the Secret One, and he will save you and
take you into Paradise."

The musicians all murmured a prayer.

Aki divided the rice ball with Yoshi and Kai and put a
fragment in her mouth. She shivered as she swallowed it.
All the tastes in the world seemed embodied in its sticky
grains, blood and bone, bitterness, salt and sweetness.

Slowly the boat made its way along the eastern coast of the lake until they came to the small town of Aomizu. Kai became something of a favorite with the musicians. They gave her a drum—she was sensitive to vibration and rhythm and she played with a natural talent. She began spending more time with the musicians, leaving Yoshi bored and restless. When he tried to order her around, the musicians teased him, calling him princeling and little lord. Several times Aki thought he was on the point of telling them who he was and she became even more eager to get him away. As she was getting ready to leave, one of the female drummers came to her and said, "We will miss you and your lute—we've never heard anything like it, any of us—and we hope you will come back one day. But we have a favor to ask: leave the little girl here. If you are dedicated to the shrine and your brother is to become a monk, what will happen to her? Rinrakuji will not accept her since she is blemished, nor will Lady Fuji take her on. But we accept her, we already love her. She has a divine gift. Heaven must have sent her to us."

"I would gladly," Aki said. "But my little brother is devoted to her. I don't think he'll leave without her."

The girl smiled slightly. "We will arrange something."

The boat had docked. Aki had the lute in her hand and their clogs ready when Yoshi came up to her, looking distressed.

"They say Kai is too sick to travel with us," he said.

Aki went immediately to where Kai was lying under

the canopy in the stern of the boat, the ritual box next to her. She seemed to have been stricken by a sudden fever. Her eyes were dilated, her skin burning.

"It is just lake fever," the musicians said. "We'll look after her. She will be recovered in a day or two."

"We can't go without her," Yoshi said, his voice trembling.

"Do you remember my father saying you must obey me in everything?" Aki replied.

"Yes, but—"

"Obedience means not saying *but*," she rebuked him. "We must go now. The boat has to leave and we must get to Rinrakuji. Kai obviously can't come with us. You'll see her again, but now you have to be strong."

He opened his mouth and she thought he was going to argue or scream, but then he bit his lip, knelt next to Kai, and stroked her hair. When he stood and let Aki take her hand he was fighting back tears.

"I am glad she is staying," Fuji said. "It is a good thing for her, and it means you are more likely to come back to us."

Aki thanked her and then asked, "Who was the old man who shared food with us at Majima?" She had not been able to stop thinking about him.

"Everyone just calls him Father; he is a traveling priest of some sort. The musicians belong to the same faith. He usually waits for the boats at the markets. They look forward to his blessing. Maybe one day they will tell you the story of the Secret One. It is very strange and moving."

Aki found she longed to hear it, but now there was no

time. The boat was preparing to move on. She stared briefly across the lake toward Nishimi, her childhood home, lost in the haze. Then she took Genzo in its carrying cloth and stepped from the side of the boat onto the wooden dock. She had her bow on her back, no longer feeling the need to hide it. Yoshi was passed across to her. Cries of farewell and thanks rang between boat and shore.

The ropes were cast off and the sail raised. Aki and Yoshi watched and waved for several moments, then turned away and began to follow the steep, narrow road that climbed through the mountains to Rinrakuji.

18

SHIKANOKO

Through the courtyards at Ryusonji echoed the voices of singers, accompanied by lute players and by the old blind man, who, it was said, had once been a sorcerer but had lost his powers along with his eyes. He must have had some natural talent, for he had learned the notes and words swiftly in the course of the winter.

They had new songs to sing, about the victory of the Miboshi and the flight of the Kakizuki, poignant, stirring tales of courage in battle and nobility in defeat, of the shocking but necessary death of Prince Momozono, who had dared to rebel against his dying father, and the virtues of his younger brother, who was now Emperor Daigen.

Shika imagined that it brought the Prince Abbot great pleasure to hear daily the recounting of his triumph, by his former rival, now fallen into senility. He was uncle to the new emperor, and the Kakizuki, his old enemies, were in exile. The wives and children they had left behind were slaughtered, their palaces were rebuilt and occupied by the victorious Miboshi, their presence was being erased from the capital as though they had not dominated its life, its customs, its arts and fashions for nearly fifty years.

Yet Shika knew the prelate was not as satisfied as he might have been. Two things irked him, two missing bodies. The heads of the defeated were displayed on bridges and along the riverbank, but Kiyoyori's was not among them. The Prince Abbot's men had combed through the wreckage of the palace and the surrounding streets. The corpses of Momozono and his wife were identified in the piles of dead, along with those of their retinue, male and female, who had died in the fighting or the fire, but Kiyoyori's body had not been discovered nor had that of Yoshimori, only son of the former Crown Prince.

It was reported that Kiyoyori had been last seen in front of the New Shining Hall. An arrow had pierced him and an unknown man who had dashed in front of him. Both had fallen into the flames just before the roof collapsed. Kiyoyori could not have survived, eyewitnesses said, but because his body had not been found, fanciful tales had begun to spread about him, the most popular being that the dragon child of Ryusonji had carried him away to join his son, Tsumaru, who, it was rumored, had been kidnapped by the Prince Abbot, had died in some mysterious way, and was now a manifestation of that same dragon.

Shika knew from his own experience that men hate above all those they have wronged, and the Prince Abbot's hatred for Kiyoyori had grown even more bitter since the discovery of Tsumaru's body in the lake. He blamed the child's father for the bungled rescue attempt at the same time as he resented Kiyoyori's spirited refusal to be coerced. The suggestion that Ryusonji's own divine being might have aided him in some way was intolerable. The Prince Abbot attempted to suppress the rumors and the tales; his secret police cut out people's tongues for repeating them.

Shika had spent at least part of every day throughout the winter with the Prince Abbot. For many of those days he had been required to fast, subjected to ordeals of icy water, and deprived of sleep. Slowly, under these stern disciplines, the natural power of the mask had been controlled. He had been taught words of power, some from sutras, others known only to the Prince Abbot, Gessho, and a few older monks. With the aid of all these things, the mask took him to places beyond the human world, where the spirit of the deer spoke to him and through him.

But every step forward demanded a price. Often he would emerge from a trance and see in the hollowed eyes and slackened faces around him vestiges of some ritual he had taken part in, without his knowledge and against his will. The mask had been made with both male and female elements; it harnessed the regenerative power of the forest, the sexual drive of the stag. All this interested the Prince Abbot deeply.

He was delighted with his progress. Shika became his new favorite, replacing the young monk Eisei, who had been so burned by the mask. Eisei recovered from his injuries but would always be disfigured. He wore a black silk covering across his face, behind which his eyes burned with despair.

Shika went every day to sit with Sesshin. The old man did not seem to recognize him, but smiled at him gratefully and patted his hand. The Prince Abbot often questioned him about Sesshin, but even when Shika was in trances induced by strong potions, the power that Sesshin had transferred to him remained hidden. It would reveal itself, Shika thought, when it was ready and when he was.

The Prince Abbot also questioned him about Kiyoyori. "That scoundrel has become more popular since he died than he ever was when he was alive," he complained. "What magic arts did he possess to vanish without a trace? Did the sorceress come for him? Could she have flown into the burning building and carried him away?"

Shika had learned that many of the Prince Abbot's questions did not require an immediate answer. He did not reply now, but he was thinking about how Lady Tora had visited Shisoku's hut in some supernatural manner during the making of the mask.

The Prince Abbot was watching him intently. Shika looked away toward the garden. It was the beginning of the fourth month, a warm day with more than a little humidity in the air. Outside the sun shone glaringly on the wisteria and the azaleas, giving their flowers an intense hue.

The waters of the lake rippled suddenly, a sign that the dragon child was awake, was aware of everything.

Did it remain a child, he wondered, or was it growing to its full size secretly, and would one day emerge? When he looked back into the room his vision was distorted by circles of light and dark.

"And Yoshimori?" the Prince Abbot questioned. "Was he spirited away, too? Perhaps by Hidetake's daughter, the girl they call Akihime, the Autumn Princess. As long as he lives, the Kakizuki will have a cause to reunite and inspire them."

He sat in thought for a long time while the room grew warmer. Sweat began to trickle from Shika's face and chest. He longed for the cool shade of the forest, the dawn mists of the mountain. He remembered the waterfall.

The Prince Abbot's voice startled him, bringing him back suddenly. "Is that where you will find them? That place where your mind just wandered? Is it in the Darkwood? Have they fled there?"

Shika still had not learned to hide his thoughts from the Prince Abbot.

"I think I will send you after them," the Prince Abbot said slowly. "She will be heading for Rinrakuji, for she was to be a shrine maiden, but she must not get there. The werehawks will accompany you so I know where you are. Bring me Kiyoyori's head and the child's. You can do what you like with the girl, let her live or die. Ride fast. They have already been on the road for days. You must overtake them."

"I cannot go without the mask," Shika replied.

The Prince Abbot smiled. "I would never separate you

from your mask. But be aware, I have cast spells on it so I can be sure my little stag will return to me."

✳

Shika left the next morning, riding Nyorin, Risu following. He had intended to leave the mare, who was just beginning to show signs of her pregnancy, but at the last moment decided to take her, telling himself he did not trust anyone there to look after her, not daring to admit that he might never come back. He thought only of disappearing into the forest, but the mask whispered to him, reminding him of all he had learned during the winter and all there was still to learn. He was tied in some way through it to the Prince Abbot, who had become his master, but he did not fully understand how or to what extent.

The Prince Abbot had instructed him to ride north and then cut across toward the western edge of the Darkwood. He could picture it all in his mind, as if on a map: the track that led south to Shimaura, the stream that flowed from the mountains, the bandits' hut where they stored weapons and loot they had taken from travelers, for it was on the boundary of Akuzenji's territory and he had ridden all over it a year and a half ago when he had spent the summer in the service of the King of the Mountain.

With only the horses and the two werehawks for company he had many hours to recall the past and reflect on what his life had become. He found himself dwelling, in particular, on the last time he saw Hina, waiting in the garden of the house below Rokujo for her father to return.

There had been no specific reports about her, but he imagined she had been found and killed along with all the other Kakizuki children. He grieved for her and then forced himself to remember the last time he had seen her father, the expression on Kiyoyori's face when the lord had seen Shika at the Prince Abbot's side.

He considered I betrayed him; he regretted sparing my life.

The werehawks fluttered and cried around his head. When they needed to rest they sat on the mare's back, preening themselves and croaking and grumbling to each other. Risu hated them and often bucked or swung her head around to bite in an attempt to dislodge them. They fluttered upward, squawking in surprise and outrage, and then returned immediately to their roost.

Shika did not know how the Prince Abbot communicated with them, but from the first day he set his mind to understand them. How was it done? Did he have to become like a bird himself or did he have to use some deeper knowledge? Did all Nature understand itself, the pine trees and the crows, the hawfinches and the berries, the fox, the rabbit, the hare? Was there some vast web of communication that joined everything? And if so, why should men stand outside it? The stag mask must have given him access to something like that; the power of the forest, Shisoku had called it. If he wore the mask, would he understand the werehawks?

At first he thought they disliked him. After all, they had attacked him at Kumayama—he still had the scar—

and before that he had shot and killed one at Matsutani. But after a while he realized they were trying in some obscure birdlike fashion to ingratiate themselves with him, even to please him. One in particular, which had a gold feather in its left wing, often sat on his shoulder and made remarks in his ear. He called it Kon, and the other Zen, for its wicked eyes and arrogant manner reminded him of Akuzenji.

They showed him the route to follow, along the eastern edge of the lake, and every night one or other of them flew off to the south, to report back to the Prince Abbot. He resented that they were spying on him, but he knew they were not to blame for it and he treated them well, scratching their heads, feeding them the grain with which he had been supplied, listening to their strange talk, trying to decipher it. They seemed to know something about him, as though they could smell within him the sweet fiery nugget that Sesshin had fed him, and wanted to partake of it.

He meditated on that power, determined to learn how to use it, following the rhythm of the horses' pace. He noticed with his conscious mind the lush spring landscape, the fresh green of the new leaves, the flooded rice fields that reflected the sky, aware of his own youth and energy, excited by all that lay before him, glad to be free of the stifling atmosphere of Ryusonji. Farmers worked in the fields, a few monks and merchants passed along the road, all making the most of the fine days before the onset of the plum rains. There were no signs of battle. The Miboshi had confined their advance to the capital and were consolidating their conquests in the east. He wondered what had happened at Matsutani, and his own estate of Kumayama. Whose hands were they in now? Presumably his uncle had been rewarded for handing him over, and had allied himself with the victors.

One day I will get it back, he vowed.

He followed the Prince Abbot's command and rode fast, sleeping for a few hours at night in the woods, using Nyorin's saddle as a pillow. The werehawks led him away from the lakeside road, through rice fields, skirting the small town of Aomizu. He had never been here before; in the distance to the east the mountains rose, their highest peaks still snowcapped, and he knew that somewhere to the south lay the course of a stream leading him to the pass through to the Darkwood.

One afternoon he came to the road between Aomizu and Rinrakuji. It was a little before sunset. He did not know if he should turn east or west, so he let the horses graze for a while in a small grove and waited for the werehawks to show him.

Kon had flown toward the west, and suddenly returned, landed on Shika's shoulder, and said distinctly, "Prince Yoshimori!" Zen gave a triumphant squawk, flew upward from Risu's back, and settled on an overhanging branch, peering expectantly.

Shika crept toward the edge of the road, bow in hand.

Two figures were hurrying along the road from the direction of Aomizu. One was definitely a child; the other turned and looked back and he realized it was a girl, and that there were two men following her, flitting in and out of sight like wolves pursuing deer, like the wolf that had driven him to Shisoku. There was no one else around. She was running desperately now, dragging the child by the hand, tripping and stumbling. They were closing in on her.

He heard one call, "I'll take the girl; the boy is for you. Then we'll swap."

She stopped and spun around to face them. She was carrying a bundle, but she thrust it into the child's hands and pulled out a dagger. She had a small, light bow on her back.

Shika thought he could gallop past, seize the child, and escape. The girl was not important. Who the men were he had no idea; they wore no emblems, crests, or armor. But he could see their faces, their undisguised lust and greed. The girl's courage, her defiant stance, spoke to him. At that moment he decided to save her life.

He took the arrows from the quiver on his back, drew the bow, and shot rapidly twice. Both arrows found their mark, one in each naked throat. The look of astonishment, the useless clutching at the shaft, the weakening of muscles and sinews, the loss of blood, all took place in a few brief moments. Both men fell dead.

The girl turned and looked at him, her face white. She did not threaten him with the knife. It was clear she knew she had no defense against his arrows, but she drew the boy closer, the blade at his throat.

Shika saw she was planning to kill Yoshimori and then

herself. Her desperation and her resolve touched him even more deeply.

"Don't be afraid of me," he called. "I will help you."

And he felt Sesshin's power come to life within him, and knew he was going to defy the Prince Abbot.

19

HINA

Yukikuni no Takaakira was riding through the capital looking for somewhere to live. Lord of the Snow Country, he was close to Lord Miboshi Aritomo, adviser, confidant, and as much of a friend as anyone could be to that taciturn and suspicious man, who had been deeply scarred by the loss of his family and his years of exile. The Minatogura lord's temper was unpredictable, his nature unforgiving, his favor, once forfeited, lost forever. He never forgot an insult or an offense, never overlooked a mistake. Yet Takaakira respected him and even loved him, admiring his fortitude, his perseverance, and the unexpected high ideals that had led him to establish courts of law that demanded written records, title deeds to estates, signed testimonies to exploits in battle, and a system to hand out rewards fairly.

Takaakira saw, with sorrow, one beautiful house after

another reduced to ashes, shrouds of smoke still hanging over them. Perhaps alone among the Miboshi, who now occupied the capital, he regretted the destruction of the Kakizuki. As a youth he had visited the city many times and had reveled in the richness of its art, poetry, music, and dance. He admired with all his heart the flamboyant heroism of the Kakizuki warriors in the recent battle, who had sallied out to meet the Miboshi, one by one, as men used to, according to the old songs, calling out their names, demanding a worthy opponent. Under Aritomo's orders they had been brought down by a hail of arrows from an anonymous and united force. This new form of warfare had broken their spirit. They no longer understood how to fight. The men fled with Lord Keita, presumably to regroup at Rakuhara or some other stronghold in the west, abandoning their palaces and their residences, their exquisite gardens, now in the first flush of spring, and in most cases their wives and children.

Lord Aritomo, who understood the nature of both power and revenge, had ordered these to be put to death. Takaakira had admired his lord's ruthlessness while deeply regretting the extinguishing of young, innocent lives. And that, he reflected, was an essential part of his nature. He admired so easily—human qualities of courage or kindness, artistic talent, the beauty of nature, all the poignancy of existence expressed in poetry—and he felt loss so deeply, sometimes unbearably. He was riven by the sadness of things, and these days, in the defeated city, had been more raw and unendurable than anything he had experienced in his life. He had never felt so agonizingly alive, never longed so much for the indifference and tranquillity of death.

The slaughter, now, was mostly over. Aritomo had moved into Lord Keita's palace, which had survived undamaged. Preparations were under way for the crowning of the new emperor. Courts were being set up to share out the spoils of war. Miboshi elders were moving into official positions formerly occupied by their Kakizuki counterparts. Takaakira was one of these; his title now was Senior Counselor of the Left, but before he could begin carrying out his duties he had to find a house.

On the edge of the city, below Rokujo, on the western side, he came upon a wall around a garden, neglected but, to his eye, not unpleasing. Wildflowers and long grass grew around the gate, which stood half-open, covered in morning glory vines. He dismounted and gave the reins of his horse to his companion, Gensaku, and walked quietly inside.

A long, low building of excellent proportions stood on his left, looking out to the southwest. The garden was overgrown, the shrubs straggling, the pebbles and the pond choked with weeds. A cat had been sunning itself on a large, flat rock near the house. At the sound of his footsteps it lifted its head, leaped from the rock, and vanished under the veranda.

Apart from the cat, there did not seem to be a single living being. Dust lay, mostly undisturbed, on the veranda. He noticed the cat's paw prints and, lit by the afternoon sun, a child's. He felt regret. He did not want to shed blood in the place he had already decided he was going to take for his own. He considered calling Gensaku and waiting outside until the deed was done, but something prevented him. He stepped inside.

He could not see anyone, all the shutters were closed and the interior dark, but he thought he could hear the child's light tread as it flitted from room to room. The pursuit excited him; it was like a childhood game. Finally he could see its eyes, shining in the half-light like a cat's. He had cornered it. He grabbed it. It made no resistance; in fact, it seemed to be clutching something, its hands were not free. It did not cry out or struggle as he carried it out onto the veranda. He must call Gensaku and have him take it away and put it to death.

On the veranda the sunlight fell on a girl's face. She looked at him with a grave, resigned expression, but she did not speak. When had she last eaten? he wondered. She was holding a box in both hands and under her arm a folded text. He pried open her hands and took the box, but when he went to open it she said sternly, "No!"

He put the box down and took the text from her. It seemed to be a treatise on herbs and medicine, esoteric perhaps. His interest was piqued. He had read all the works of the yin-yang masters and had dabbled a little in secret arts.

"Why do you have this?" he asked.

She sighed in a way so knowing and so mature, he was surprised and touched. *She knows she will die. Yet she can-*

not be more than ten years old. How can one so young be so adult and so aware?

At that moment he seemed to be shown all the years of her life as they might have been: growing up, learning to read and write, becoming a woman, marrying. Was all that going to be extinguished in a moment on his orders? And then he saw the alternative: he would save her. It was so simple, it almost made him gasp; simple and perfect. She would be Murasaki to his Genji. He had always dreamed of having a child he would bring up, like a daughter, to become a wife, a companion who shared his interests, who would be his equal in intellect and learning, who would love him. He imagined the clothes he would dress her in, the books he would give her, the games of incense matching and the poetry that he would teach her.

"What is your name? Don't be afraid of me. I'm not going to hurt you. I'll never let anyone hurt you, I promise."

She continued to regard him unwaveringly, then the ghost of a smile flickered over her lips.

Takaakira thought, *She trusts me*, and a feeling of joy came over him.

"Tell me your name," he urged.

"I don't have a grown-up name," she said. "Everyone's always called me Hina."

"That's charming. And your father's name?"

"I don't remember."

It would be easy enough to find out. But on second thought it might be better not to know. If she was from some high-ranking or important Kakizuki family it would mean a far more serious act of disobedience on his part. He guessed her family were provincial warriors who kept a residence in the capital but lived on their country estate. The house was pleasant but not grand, on the west side and too far from the Imperial Palace to be fashionable— and luckily for him, hidden from prying eyes.

"Stay here," he told Hina, and went to the gate to give instructions to Gensaku, to find serving women and cleaners, to put one of his men in charge of running the household, and to buy food, tea, and wine. Then he added casually, "There was a girl hiding in the house. Her father died fighting for us and she fled here. I will look after her for the time being until we can find her family. But there's no need to spread this widely."

Gensaku bowed his head and designated one of his soldiers to inspect the house and find out what was needed.

Takaakira returned to the veranda. Hina had placed the box on the floor and was kneeling before it, her lips moving in prayer as if she were thanking it. A slight chill came over him; there was something uncanny about her, as if she were a fox wife or had fallen from the stars. Yet this only made her more appealing to him.

When he approached her she sat back on her heels and smiled at him. It was a little hesitant, but nonetheless it was a true smile.

"Father promised to teach me to read," she said. "But he has not returned."

"I don't think he ever will," Takaakira said quietly, grieving for a man he had not known, an enemy.

The smile faded and her eyes shone with tears.

"I will teach you," he said, and while he waited for the house to be made ready he began to show her the characters, tracing them with his finger in the dust on the floor.

20

TAMA

In Minatogura, Lady Tama waited anxiously for news. Life in the convent was tranquil, but she was bored and restless. She worried about the children, she longed for Matsutani, homesick for its fields and streams and the mountains that encircled it. She wondered if the damage from the earthquake had been repaired, if the lake had been refilled, who was overseeing the preparation of the rice fields and the raising of seedlings, the airing of clothes, the springcleaning. She was certain that only she would do it properly.

She had seen the Miboshi army depart, thousands of them, some by road, some by boat, and, though no one had told her directly, she assumed Masachika had gone with them. If Matsutani and Kuromori fell he would be there to declare them his, by right of conquest, and probably by right of law as well. She had found out his claim had not yet been heard. The tribunal, made up of old men who had retired from the battlefield, was still working through cases, trying to clear the backlog before the victories of the new campaign brought a fresh flood of demands for legal recognition.

"We heard last night that Lord Miboshi has taken possession of the capital," the Abbess told her one morning. "It seems the Kakizuki incited the Crown Prince to rebel against his father; he was killed in the fighting and many Kakizuki, too. The rest fled. The Emperor has passed away and his second son will succeed to the throne. We will observe a period of mourning and pray for the spirits of the departed."

She spoke calmly, but Tama could sense her distress.

"If only men truly followed the way of the Enlightened One," she went on, half to herself. "If they shunned ambition and the lust for power, refused to take life, and were content with what they had, they would not unleash waves of suffering on the world."

Tama bowed her head to show agreement but could not help asking, "Is there any word of our thief?"

"It was he who brought me this news."

"So where is he now? Why did you not tell me at once?" She could not hide her impatience.

"Your time here has not altered your determination to claim your estate?"

"I am more determined than ever, but I am afraid it is all too late. I must speak with Hisoku."

"Stay here with us," the Abbess pleaded. "Abandon your claim and find peace."

"If Hisoku has returned without the deeds, I will have to. But if I have documentary evidence I intend to present it to the court."

The Abbess sighed. "Go to the pavilion. I will send him to you."

❋

Hisoku bowed to the ground before Tama and then they sat knee to knee on the small veranda. The cherry blossoms had all fallen and the tree's green leaves gave a dappled shade. Her heart was beating a little faster from his presence and she suspected his might be, too. She had no intention of becoming intimate with him—she would not risk her reputation—but the knowledge that he was attracted to her was reassuring. It meant he would do anything for her.

From the breast of his robe he drew out a small package and placed it on the ground between them.

"You found them without any difficulty?"

"Lady," he said, "I don't know how much you have heard . . ."

"Tell me everything."

"When I came to your estate at Matsutani, Lord Kiyoyori and his daughter had already left for the capital."

"Kiyoyori left? I thought he would stay and fight for the estates. I imagined, if Matsutani were taken, he would retreat to Kuromori, which could be defended indefinitely."

"That is what his men have done, apparently. Matsutani had been damaged by the earthquake and the garrison left there had no hope of taking on the Miboshi. They fled and are holed up in Kuromori."

"Waiting for Kiyoyori to appear, I suppose. Where is he?"

"It is assumed he died with Prince Momozono, but it is not confirmed."

She felt unexpected grief well up within her. Ah, she would never see him again, her husband of seven years, the father of her son!

"And the children?"

Hisoku had been speaking in a dry, unemotional tone, but now his voice faltered. "All Kakizuki children in the capital were sought out and killed. Again there is no confirmation, there were so many and they were so young. Most of the corpses were burned without being identified."

The bright day went dark and she could see nothing.

"Lady Tama? Are you going to faint? Let me call someone."

"No," she said. "Finish your account."

"All I have just told you, I heard by report. I have not been as far as the capital myself. I wanted to hurry back with your documents. Matsutani was deserted. The guards fled long before the Miboshi arrived."

"Was it the damage from the earthquake? I did not think it was so bad—surely it can all be repaired?"

"It was not the earthquake," Hisoku said. "Rebuilding had already begun. Sawn planks were stacked up in piles, cut to the right lengths and ready to put up. But there were no workmen, no guards, no servants. I saw some farmers working in the rice fields, so I went to question them. They told me the residence had fallen under the influence of evil spirits; one of them who fancied himself an expert on these matters explained that Master Sesshin must have put them in place to protect Matsutani, but since his departure they had felt abandoned and neglected and had turned spiteful. It seems two men, a guard and a carpenter, had heard their names called in Lord Kiyoyori's voice and had run into the building only to be crushed beneath falling beams, dislodged with great force from the roof. Witnesses said they heard laughter and one even claimed to have seen the spirits crouched in the rafters. After that no one dared go in the building. The shrine priest came and conducted a divination from which he concluded the spirits were beyond his capacity to deal with and should be left alone until Sesshin or some other master could exorcise them."

"I accused him of being a sorcerer," Tama said, "but I had not realized he was so powerful."

"The priest told me you had his eyes put out and sent him away into the Darkwood." His voice expressed no emotion that she could discern. She did not want to dwell on memories of that terrible day. What did it all matter now? Her son was dead, her home cursed.

"You should have killed me as you were ordered to when you came before," she cried, and tears began to fill her eyes. "Kill me now and put an end to my suffering." She could no longer hold in her feelings and for many minutes she wept bitterly.

Finally, Hisoku spoke with some hesitation. "As I said, Lady Tama, I found the documents."

"You went into the house? You weren't afraid?"

"A little afraid, yes, but very respectful. I spent several days talking with the spirits. I brought them placatory offerings, spring flowers, rice wine, and so on. I know a little about these things—my father was a gardener at the Great Shrine in Miyako and often had to soothe spirits that were displaced or offended by garden works."

"You really do have many talents," Tama said.

"In my line of work, when I have so many enemies, I don't need hostile spirits as well. I try to keep them on my side. Eventually I told the spirits I had to collect something from inside the house and they let me in. The documents were where you told me, in the cavity in the well in the kitchen."

She did not look at the package. "It is all my fault," she said. "I have destroyed the place I love. If I had not treated Master Sesshin so cruelly, if I had not turned him away, he would still be protecting my house. I did not know he had been doing it for so many years. I thought it was thanks to Heaven's blessing, Kiyoyori's ability, my own efforts. But, in truth, it was not Sesshin I was punishing. It was my husband. He started it all by bringing another woman into my house. Jealousy of her, and fear for my son when he was snatched away, made me act so cruelly and unwisely."

"You must have loved your son very much."

"I did not know how much."

"And his father, too?"

"That is no concern of yours." In fact, Tama was amazed at how strong and painful was her grief for Kiyoyori.

"From all accounts," Hisoku said, "he was a better man than his brother. Well, you yourself admitted as much to me when you said Lord Kiyoyori would have come to kill you himself, rather than send an assassin like me."

"Where is his brother, Masachika, now?" Tama said slowly. She was going to have to fight Masachika in the courts for Matsutani. But she found within her a determination to do it. She would rebuild and restore her home and make it the safe and beautiful place it had been when Kiyoyori, Hina, and Tsumaru were alive.

"He accompanied the Miboshi forces into the capital," Hisoku replied. "I heard he fought with distinction at Shimaura and the Sagigawa. Now he is assisting Lord Aritomo with the reassignment of official positions. He has been made a captain of the guard of the right."

"One brother's fortune rises while the other's falls," Tama said. "Their father wanted to have one son on each side, so that no matter who prevailed, Kuromori would stay in their family and their line would survive. He was farsighted, I suppose. But he never took into account that Matsutani was mine and still is. I will make one final effort to claim it, and if the judgment goes against me I will become a nun and pray that the departed will forgive me."

Hisoku was staring at her with open admiration. "I will help you in any way I can."

21

MASACHIKA

Masachika himself watched the Prince Abbot's men go through the ruins of Momozono's palace. He wanted to be sure Kiyoyori was dead and he wanted to give his remains a proper burial, to pacify his spirit and put an end to the conflict and rivalry their father's decision had caused between them. People were already talking about the return of the murdered Crown Prince as a vengeful ghost, and priests gathered every day at the site of his death in elaborate attempts to placate him. Their chants and the smoke of incense were the background accompaniment to Masachika's restless searching and waiting.

If anyone were to return as a vengeful ghost, he thought, surely it would be Kiyoyori. Even though no trace of his corpse was discovered, he concluded he must be dead—it was what he wanted to believe—and ordered the priests to add Kiyoyori's name to their prayers. No one told him the rumors that Kiyoyori had been rescued somehow; they did not want their tongues torn out.

Masachika went to the old house below Rokujo, but found the doors guarded and was told it had been taken over by Yukikuni no Takaakira. There was no arguing with that. Takaakira was too close to Lord Aritomo, and Masachika had no intention of making an enemy of him. He had never cared for the house anyway. It was where their mother had died and it held only sorrowful memories for him. Tsumaru was already dead, he learned, and Hina must have also perished. He had never seen his brother's son, and had last set eyes on Hina when she was an infant. Naturally, he felt some twinges of grief for them, and for the brother he had known before the rift. Memories of their shared boyhood rose fresh in his mind: their horses, their hawks, their first bows and swords. They had been close friends then; he had admired Kiyoyori deeply, and sought his approval in everything, until he had grown old enough to realize his unenviable position as a younger son. Then he had begun to resent the brother who, by accident of birth, had everything while Masachika had nothing. His marriage, his wife's brother's unexpected death, had seemed to redress fortune's balance in his favor until his father's brutal decision had taken away his wife and his estate and bestowed them on Kiyoyori.

He had gone to Minatogura burning with resentment and rage, but he had mastered his feelings and served his new family, the Yamada, and his new lords, the Miboshi, diligently. He had seen how he must make himself useful to those around him to survive, and he had become adept at willingly performing tasks no one else wanted to do.

He had obeyed his father, as sons were supposed to, and now he intended to enjoy the fruits of his obedience. He was even grateful now to his father, who had ensured his position on the winning side. Matsutani and Kuromori were now his, with or without the tribunal's ruling. He was the only surviving heir.

Yet he did not feel secure. He began to fear that the estates might be bestowed on someone else, that Lord Aritomo might forget him or overlook him, that his Kakizuki blood might count against him. When it was reported that the last of Kiyoyori's men were holding out in Kuromori he requested permission to lead an attack on them before the rains set in.

He was given a hundred warriors, who had been waiting restlessly in the city for their next chance for a battle, a skirmish, or a siege—anything was better than hunting down women and children. They were eager for a chance to prove themselves again. Most had no land and were hungry for recognition and rewards. Masachika and his second in command, Yasuie, could both read and write and, even before they left Miyako, were beset with requests to record the men's names, their war history, the battles they had fought in, the wounds they had received.

It amused Masachika and he found it a useful means to learn each individual history and form judgments on this loosely associated troop of men who were only in the vaguest terms under his command. Some were braggarts, some brave (and of course it was possible to be both), some pragmatic and calculating. They were content to follow him for the time being, if only because he had some legitimacy: he was taking back what was his and he knew the country and the terrain, but each man would be fighting for his own glory and gain.

On the second evening, they arrived at the Shimaura barrier. It was still decorated with the heads of Kiyoyori's men who had died defending it in vain. Masachika himself had killed more than one of them. He had not thought about it in the heat of the battle, but now he felt uneasy. They had been his family's retainers. He had been taught by the older men, had grown up with the younger ones. Their sightless eye sockets (the eyes had already been pecked out by crows) seemed to reproach him. He would have liked to have the heads taken down and buried, yet he did not dare show weakness or any sympathy for the Kakizuki. Instead he addressed the dead boldly, by name, mocking them, making the living laugh heartily.

He slept badly that night, woke the others before daybreak, and rode with a somber heart toward Matsutani.

The sun rose over the eastern mountains, dazzling their eyes. Ahead, slightly to the north, lay the Darkwood. On the flat land along the river the young rice plants glowed a brilliant green, swaying above their reflections in the flooded fields. Frogs croaked from the banks and butterflies flew up from the grass. The air was moist and heavy, the men sweated beneath their armor, the horses' coats turned dark.

In the early afternoon they approached Matsutani. Sensing they were near their destination, the men began to break away to collect whatever food they could find: some eggs here, a bucket of millet there, fresh greens pulled from the earth. The farmers and their families did not protest or resist, but stared resentfully in Masachika's direction. He wondered if they recognized him. He wanted to say, "I am your lord. Everything here is mine."

Yasuie was eyeing him curiously. "There's some strange history, isn't there, between you and your brother?"

"Nothing that need concern anyone, anymore, since my brother is dead."

"Just seems a bit unusual that you ended up on opposite sides."

Masachika urged his horse on, making no answer, but when he arrived at the west gate, alone, he called in a loud voice, "I am Kuromori no Jiro no Masachika. I have come to reclaim my estate."

Yasuie caught up with him. "The men were told the house is occupied by evil spirits. That's why it is deserted. They were placed there as guardians by the old man Sesshin."

"Sesshin?" Masachika said in surprise. "My father's old fool? Well, no wonder they've gone bad."

"They say it happened after the lady had his eyes put out."

Masachika said, hiding a shudder, "It is a feeble excuse for failing to carry out any repairs. I heard there was an earthquake, months ago. It's disgraceful that nothing has been done." He dismounted and let the horse graze. He walked through the gate and spoke again in a loud voice. "It is I, Masachika, lord of Kuromori and Matsutani."

There was a long moment of silence, long enough for Masachika to observe the destruction and neglect of the once beautiful house and garden. The lake was a stretch of mud, the summer pavilion a pile of charred wood. Then a ripple of laughter came from inside the half-burned residence.

"Masachika, come here!"

"Kiyoyori?" he gasped. "Brother?"

Yasuie spoke behind him. "Don't go any closer. It is not your brother. It cannot be."

"I'd know his voice anywhere," Masachika said, and stepped toward the veranda.

An iron pot hurtled toward him. He ducked his head to the side just in time. The pot struck him on the shoulder, knocking him to his knees.

A mocking voice, nothing like Kiyoyori's, came from the house, saying, "Your brother's wife is the Matsutani lady, and your brother is the Kuromori lord. What are you, Masachika? Neither Kakizuki nor Miboshi, you are nothing!"

More shrieks of laughter followed, as the spirits hurled out kitchen utensils and household objects, a bamboo dipper, two small brooms, a lacquer tray, and several quite valuable bowls, which smashed to pieces on the path.

"It must be some local urchins," Masachika said furiously. "I'll cut off their ears; I'll sell them to the silver mines."

This threat only caused more hilarity among the spirits.

Masachika had retreated out of range back to the gate. Behind him he could hear that the men had regrouped. They were probably waiting, with callous curiosity, to see what he would do next. His authority was slipping away. He called out, "Who will drive these brats from my house?"

No one moved or spoke.

"What? Are you all afraid?"

Yasuie said at his side, "They are afraid of no one human. Beings from another world, that's another matter."

A young man appeared in the gateway. He was of huge size, a head taller than Masachika, and carried a long spear heavier than most men could lift. He was Yasuie's younger brother, Yasunobu.

"I will get rid of them for you, Lord Masachika."

"Brother, don't go in there," Yasuie said. "No one will despise you."

"But I would despise myself," the youth said, his voice light. "Now I have offered, I must—or allow my name to be remembered as a coward's."

Holding his spear out in front of him, he ran to the veranda and leaped inside. There came two fierce shrieks followed by a howl of pain. Yasunobu came flying out from the house, pierced through the stomach by his own spear. He fell with such force he was nailed to the ground.

Yasuie and Masachika ran to him, but there was nothing to be done. His life's blood was pouring from him. As they tried to pry the spear from the ground a rain of small insects like bees fell around their heads, stinging them on their faces and hands, each sting an intense spark of pain. But Yasuie would not leave his brother, whose screams were subsiding into a ragged panting, and Masachika felt he could not retreat without him.

Finally, the spear came loose and, as Yasuie eased it out, Yasunobu's panting ceased. They lifted the body between them and carried it beyond the gate. Once they were outside the walls, the insects left them. Masachika could feel his face swelling, his eyes closing up.

He glanced up at the sun, its rays making his face ache even more. A few hours of daylight still remained. He must act to remove the humiliation the spirits had inflicted on him. He would go at once to Kuromori. The only hope of succeeding was in a surprise attack from behind, down the steep slope of the mountain at the rear of the fortress. The defenders would not be expecting that. He would go immediately before any reckless farmer thought to warn them.

Yasuie wept beside the corpse, tears oozing from eyes that had closed to slits.

"Stay and bury him," Masachika said. "The rest of you come with me. We will take Kuromori, and then we will return and deal with whatever evil it is that has possessed this place."

There was a slight murmur from the men, not quite grumbling or dissent. Masachika said, "If anyone prefers squatting here sucking eggs to battle, he can help Yasuie bury his brother. All names will be recorded, those who stay and those who come with me."

All except Yasuie went with him. He led them up the valley, along the stream that flowed from the Darkwood and had once filled the lake at Matsutani. As they left the estate, Masachika recalled the day he had married Tama, the thrill of having a young, beautiful wife, the shock of her brother's death, how he had consoled her, rejoicing silently that Matsutani would now be his. And then the nightmare as the two old men, their fathers, put their monstrous plan into practice.

Kiyoyori, to his credit, had tried to persuade them to abandon it, had remonstrated with his father, persisting even in the face of the old man's terrifying rage. But if Kiyoyori had succeeded in making them change their minds, Masachika would still be Kakizuki, and he would probably now be dead or in flight. He had been given a second chance. If he could take Kuromori, both estates would be his. The pain in his hands and face did not let him forget that Matsutani was haunted, but he did not dwell on it. He would find some sorcerer or other to get rid of the spirits, and in the meantime, no one else would be able to snatch his jewel from him.

He followed tracks he had often galloped along with his brother. How many hours of their lives had they spent exploring the forest and the mountain? Throughout their boyhood they had devised strategies to attack and defend the fortress that was their home, and had practiced endlessly for their adult life as warriors, with their bows, swords, and horses.

Now, as he and his men rode farther into the forest, he

ran through those strategies. They would ascend the mountain behind the fortress and drop down on it from above, as if from the heavens. But, to avoid lookouts and guards, they must leave the stream and strike out to the north, turning east once they were past Kuromori.

He was sure this made sense, yet his mind was clouding as though he had a fever, and he was having trouble seeing. The terrain was rough, scattered with boulders, and very steep. The horses quickened their pace into a clumsy canter, stumbling and plunging. When they reached the small plateau where they would turn east, they were breathing hard and sweating more than ever. A couple had grazed their knees and blood oozed through the hair.

Masachika did not allow any rest but led them on at a gallop. Between the trunks of the pine trees the last rays of the sun threw their speeding shadows before them. Then the red orb slipped behind the western mountains, turning the sky vermilion. The white moon in the east slowly became silver.

By the time they came to the top of the crag above the fortress, it was close to nightfall. Below them, smoke rose from fires and a few lamps gleamed. It was impossible to tell how many men held the fortress and too dark to see if the northern side was defended. But he would not wait till dawn; the chances of being discovered were too great. He had forbidden the men from speaking since the time they had left the plateau, but no one could keep a horse from neighing.

He allowed himself a moment to peer down on Kuromori, now at last within his grasp. Ignoring the pain and the fact that he could hardly see, he made a sign that the men should follow him, and led the way over the edge of the cliff.

There was a path of sorts, just as he remembered, made by foxes or deer. He and Kiyoyori had followed a stag down it, a lifetime ago. The horses crashed down, some squealing in fear while their riders whooped and shouted.

Masachika was in front, but his sight was darkening, and then he realized he could not breathe. His throat was closing. He gasped and choked. *It is the bees*, he thought, *They have poisoned me.* His horse stumbled and he went over its head. He was aware of his face in the dirt, of his body struggling for breath, and then a hoof struck him on the back of his head and he lost consciousness.

22

AKI

Aki tried not to look at the dead men and instead stared at the bowman and the two horses as they trotted toward her. She had to decide in seconds whether to cut Yoshi's throat and then her own or to trust the stranger when he said he would help her. Then she saw the werehawks and knew at once what they were and whom they served—the man her father had hated and feared above all others. One bird was already flying south to tell its master that the fugitive emperor was found. It was time to step into the river of death.

But the birds distracted her, drawing her eyes toward them, making her hesitate. The other bird was now swooping after the first. It seemed faster and larger. She expected to see them both disappear in the direction of the capital, but the second bird caught up with the other and attacked it, striking with its beak and attempting to grasp it with its talons. Both birds were shrieking and a flurry of black feathers fell, swirling, bloodstained, to the ground.

Then the horses, white stallion, brown mare, reached her, and the rider leaped down.

He took the knife from her, with a movement so swift and sure she had no defense against it, and he whistled to the birds, as a hunter calls his falcons. One returned to his shoulder, the other fluttered to the ground a little way off. The man went to it and picked it up, carrying it back gently. Its eyes glazed and it went limp. He knelt, stroking its black feathers, his face intent.

The remaining werehawk had fluttered from his shoulder to the ground and now bowed its head to its dead fellow. Tears seemed to glisten in its eyes and it spoke in a broken voice that Aki did not understand. Then it hopped to where Yoshi was still hiding behind her, stood in front of him, and bobbed its head three times.

"Kon killed Zen," the man said. "I did not expect that. He wanted to stop him returning to the capital."

"They are werehawks," Aki said. "In the service of the Prince Abbot at Ryusonji. You understand their speech, they obey you—or one of them does—so you must serve the Prince Abbot, too."

"I did," he said slowly. "But Kon tells me this boy is the Emperor, and you are the Autumn Princess."

She stared at him. He was tall and lean, with thick black hair tied up like a warrior's. He looked as though he had been sleeping in the woods, his face slightly stubbled, and dark, either from the sun or dirt. But his skin was smooth, his features pleasing, his leaf-shaped eyes deep black.

"I was known as the Autumn Princess," she said. "Aki-hime, people used to call me, in the capital."

"And people call me Shikanoko or Shika. My name used to be Kazumaru, but I am no longer a child and I do not have an adult name."

"Shikanoko? The deer's child? Why are you called that?"

She felt quite calm and unafraid now. She wanted him to keep talking to her. She liked the sound of his voice. She wanted to trust him. Then she remembered the dead men, the swift, unhesitating killing, the werehawk.

Shikanoko said, "I will tell you as we ride." He knelt before Yoshi. "I am going to lift Your Majesty onto this mare, Risu. Akihime will ride behind you and hold you."

Genzo sounded a warning, thrumming note.

"I must not be called Majesty," the child said, "only Yoshi. I must not tell anyone who I am." He leaned against Aki, shrinking away from Shika. "Does what you said mean my father and grandfather are dead?"

"They have gone to the next world and are awaiting their rebirth," Aki told him. "My father is there, too, and my mother."

"And my mother?"

"When we get to the temple we will pray for their spirits," Aki said.

The child did not reply, but tears began to trickle down

his cheeks. He cried silently. The mare swung her head around and nuzzled him as if he were her foal.

"Kai," he whimpered. "I want Kai."

Aki said to Shika, "We were heading for Rinrakuji. My father told me we would find shelter there."

"And then what? Sooner or later the Miboshi will attack that temple and the Emperor will be discovered."

"Nevertheless, first we must go to Rinrakuji. I must obey my father."

"Very well," Shika said. "I will take you there. But it's almost dark. Don't you want to rest a little, you and the child?"

"The moon is almost full and will be rising soon. Surely we can get to the temple before it sets?"

Shika did not say anything more, but lifted Yoshi onto the mare's back, made a rein from the lead rope, and told Yoshi to hold on to it.

"You don't need to lift me," Aki said. "Make a stirrup with your hand and I can jump up."

He did as she said. Risu had made no objection to the child, but she swung her hindquarters away when Aki tried to mount. Aki slipped down into Shika's arms. For a moment she felt his body against hers, his hands holding her. Then he muttered an apology and stepped back, giving Risu a smack on her shoulder.

"Stand still!"

"I am not dressed for riding!" Aki hitched up her robe, baring her legs like a farm girl. "I'll try again. I'll be ready for her this time."

The mare's coat was smooth against her skin, her flesh warm. Aki put her arms around Yoshi and held the rope with one hand. Shika leaped onto the stallion's back and Kon flew up to his shoulder.

"What about those men?" Aki said as they rode off. "Do we just leave them there?"

"Let them rot," Shika replied, and then, "Who were they? Did you know them?"

"One had been following us since we left Miyako. I thought we had shaken him off, but as we left Aomizu I realized he had caught up with us."

"That's a long way to keep following someone. Did he know who you were? Why was he so persistent?"

"I think something about us had roused his lust," she said.

"What was he going to do to us?" Yoshi said.

"Don't worry about him. He is dead now and can no longer do anything, good or bad, to anyone." Aki tried to speak reassuringly, but thinking about what might have happened made her tremble. The days with the enter- tainers on the boat had awakened something in her. She remembered the suitors who had started hanging around the house in the city. Most girls her age would be married by now. She recoiled from the idea—she had made her vows of purity—yet she was drawn to it at the same time. Instead, neither a wife nor a shrine maiden, she was riding through the twilight, following a man on a white stallion who had just saved her life, the Emperor of the Eight Is- lands held tightly in her arms.

After a couple of miles they came to a crossroads. Rin-rakuji lay some way to the east, while the track between Kitakami and Shimaura ran from north to south, following a small, shallow stream, crossing and recrossing it as it wound between the mountains. The road was not much used. It was impassable in the rainy season, and people preferred to travel by boat over the lake. Now the crossroads was deserted. The mountains loomed to the east, their huge dark shapes outlined by the moonlight behind them. The wind had risen and was making the pine trees sigh and moan. The air was warm and humid and insects were calling.

The horses walked with nervous steps, and just before the meeting of the four roads they balked completely. Nothing would make them move on.

Kon flew in an upward spiral above the crossroads and then came back to Shika's shoulder, chattering quietly but urgently.

"There is a spirit there," Shika said. "The horses will not go past it."

"You are just making it up to persuade us to turn back." Aki's earlier mistrust returned.

"Not back. We must go south a little way and then we will go into the Darkwood. I know a place where no one will find you."

A voice came out of the dusk.

"Shikanoko! Is that you?"

Aki saw his face pale. "Lord Kiyoyori?" he whispered.

"Yes, it is I."

Aki could see nothing. Risu was trembling beneath her. Shika dismounted and gave the stallion's reins to her. "I'm going to talk to him."

"Who is it?"

"It is, or was, the Kuromori lord."

23

SHIKANOKO

Shika took the mask from the brocade bag and slipped it over his face. He stepped into the exact center where the four roads met and found himself in a place between worlds.

He had learned about such things from the Prince Abbot: crossroads, riverbanks, seashores, bridges, islands were all points where the worlds came together and touched, where miracles took place, where saints and restless ghosts dwelled, where adepts might be shown their next lives, or Paradise, or the different levels of Hell.

The Book of the Future, in which, the Prince Abbot claimed, neither Yoshimori's name nor that of his father were written, had been disclosed centuries before to Prince Umayado in one such place, between the worlds.

He stood on the banks of the river of death. He saw its black, still water, and heard the splash of the ferryman's oars. The moon cleared the last mountain peak and in its light he saw Kiyoyori. Pity and revulsion churned in his belly. The lord's skin was burned, his eyes sightless. As Shika went closer he saw that his chest did not move to draw in breath and there was no pulse of blood in his temple.

It was impossible that he was alive, yet he stood and spoke.

"Is that the young prince with you, the true emperor?"

"Yes, it is Yoshimori, and a girl called Akihime."

The spirit reached out a charred hand, holding a blackened, twisted sword. "I will not let you take them back to Ryusonji."

"I don't intend to. She wants to go to Rinrakuji. If that is no longer safe I will hide them in the Darkwood."

"Then I must come with you, for am I not the lord of the Darkwood, of Kuromori?"

"Can you leave this place?" Shika said, doubting it was possible.

"I am not sure. I have not been here long. I had crossed two of the three streams of the river of death, and was prepared to meet the lord of Hell, when I was told a man who wronged me had taken my token of death, given it to the ferryman, and gone on in my place. You must have known about Iida no Taro, at whose hands my son died? It was he. One arrow took us both from this world at the same instant. His guilt and regret caused him to make this offer and the lord of Hell accepted it. I was told my work on earth is not finished. While the usurpers are in power the realm cannot receive the blessings of Heaven. I have to return to the world to restore the Emperor."

"How is it done?" Shika said.

"You must summon me back, Shikanoko. I resented you when I saw you in the service of the Prince Abbot, but now I understand that you were learning from him, you were stealing from him his knowledge and power, just as you stole Akuzenji's stallion, and the werehawk that has never belonged to anyone but the Prince Abbot but now does your bidding. Heaven uses us for its purposes. Bring me back so its intentions may be fulfilled. Or must I stay here forever, neither living nor dead, a ghost of the crossroads?"

Shikanoko did not answer. He recalled spells and words of power that the Prince Abbot used in rites of secrecy and magic, the spirit-return incense, the fire, the salt. He had nothing, except the mask and something he now became more acutely aware of: Sesshin's nugget. He could feel it glowing and expanding within him until the pain became so intense it took him beyond words, beyond even thought. He thought he sensed the Prince Abbot's surprise and anger as this new power combined with all he had learned at Ryusonji and surpassed it. He saw Kiyoyori's spirit clinging to the burned husk, and then another's, a horse spirit poised at that moment to enter its mother's womb.

"I am ready," Kiyoyori said, and Shikanoko commanded the two spirits to become one.

He felt a surge of power as they obeyed him. He saw Kiyoyori's spirit leave its ruined body and float above the ground. The body dissolved away into dust. The earth shook beneath them. Shika fell as if struck by lightning.

Risu neighed wildly and Nyorin answered, their calls echoing back from the flanks of the mountains.

In the distance other horses neighed in response. The werehawk flew directly upward, its ragged wings outlined against the moon.

Shika heard it calling desperately, "Rinrakuji is in flames and the Miboshi are riding this way."

Through the silence that enveloped him, numbing his senses, Shika heard the girl's voice, urging him to get up. It sounded a long way away. He stood, groggy and sick, as if he had been hit on the head, and felt for Nyorin.

"What happened?" she was saying. "Are you hurt? Can you see?"

His hands found the stallion's shoulder and he leaned against him for a moment. Risu was circling anxiously, Aki trying to control her and hold Yoshi at the same time.

What will your foal become, Risu? He did not answer Aki, as he had no words for what had just taken place.

The moon was now fully overhead and something glittered in the dust. He stepped toward it and picked it up.

"What's that?" the girl said sharply.

"It's Lord Kiyoyori's sword."

Blackened and twisted beyond recognition, it was all that remained of the Kuromori lord.

He slipped it into his belt on his right side, took the mask from his face, and said the prayers of thanks to it before placing it in the seven-layered bag. He went back to the horses and pulled himself up onto Nyorin's back.

No one knew they were on the road. Kon was still with

him, flying down now to his shoulder and croaking in admiration. Whoever had taken Rinrakuji would probably
go on to Aomizu. He had to take Aki and Yoshi deep into
the forest.

He put the stallion into a canter. Turning his head, he
saw Aki and Risu were able to keep up. The girl was holding Yoshi tightly and the child was clutching whatever
was in the bundle. He was amazed at how well she rode.

The track toward the south ran straight for a while,
the river alongside splashing swift and white under the
moon. Now and then water birds flew up, startled at their
approach, but they saw no one human. After some time,
when the moon was starting its descent, they came to
the place Shika was looking for. A small stream joined the
river through a deep valley from the east, which led to a
pass through the mountains. It was the western extent of
Akuzenji's realm; Shika had ridden through it once or twice
with the bandits. The horses knew it, too, and crossed the
stream eagerly as if they were going home.

Aki said, on the farther bank, "Yoshi keeps falling
asleep. It's hard for me to hold him. Can we stop and rest?"

"There's a hut, it's not far. We'll let him sleep there."

It was a place Akuzenji had taken over for his scouts,
where they could watch for merchants and other travelers
on the south road. It was built against the side of the hill,
beside a large natural cave where several horses could
be hidden out of sight. Shika halted the horses a short way
from it and went forward on foot, Kon flying above him,
sending an owl swooping away on silent wings.

If owls roost there it must be deserted, Shika reasoned, and indeed the hut was empty, full of dust and cobwebs. Fear of the King of the Mountain, even if he was dead, must have kept it undisturbed. He returned to the horses and led them to the cave. Water, dripping from the roof, had filled a small hollow in the soft limestone. The horses knew it even in the dark, and drank eagerly from it.

Shika lifted Yoshi down and, holding the drowsy boy against his shoulder, reached out his other hand to Aki. She took it and swung her leg over the horse's back to jump down.

He held her for a moment longer than he needed to, and felt again the spark of desire and longing that had been awakened when she had fallen against him earlier. Could she be the one who was meant for him, the one Lady Tora had told him he was to wed? She had been brought to him by Fate; she had been present when he had defied the power of the Prince Abbot and performed an unimaginable act of spirit magic. A sense of what he might be capable had been welling up steadily within him.

It was still light enough, by the moon, to see a little. Kon flew up to the roof and sat on the ridgepole, a dark outline against the darker sky.

"Does the werehawk ever sleep?" Aki asked, stepping away from him.

"They act like ordinary birds: they eat and sleep, and as you saw, they can die. Yet they are different. They are like humans in that they plot and scheme, seek favors, and ally themselves with the powerful. Perhaps because they have language."

"Which you can understand?"

"I can understand Kon. For some reason he has attached himself to me."

"Why do you call him Kon?"

"He has one golden feather," Shika explained.

"I think he has more than one," Aki replied.

Shika glanced upward, but it was too dark to see. He stepped into the hut. There was no fire or light, but it did not seem worth the effort to make them. The night was warm and, though the moon had just set, dawn was not far away. He remembered a pile of old coverings and, feeling his way to the corner of the room, found it, pulled out two of the cloths, and put Yoshi down on the rest. The boy stretched and murmured something and then dropped into a deeper sleep. His grasp on the bundle loosened and it slipped to the floor, vibrating with a faint musical chord. Aki knelt to retrieve it.

"What is it that he carries so carefully?" Shika whispered.

"It is the lute Genzo," Aki replied. "It is an imperial heirloom. It is magical. It can play by itself, if it wants to, and can change its appearance. Here, see how it looks, if it reveals itself to you."

"It is too dark to see anything," Shika replied, but Aki had already removed the lute from the bundle.

The mother-of-pearl gleamed like moonlight. Aki touched the strings and the lute began to play quietly, an old song Shika recognized, a love song.

He knelt beside her. "You can lie down and sleep, too. I will wake you when it is daylight."

She lay down and pulled the old quilt over her. "It smells," she said. "I suppose it is full of fleas, too."

He heard the note of unease, almost of fear, in her voice. "You mustn't be afraid of me," he said.

"It's not that I'm afraid of you," she replied, so softly he could hardly make out her words. "Not in the ordinary way. Maybe I am afraid of myself, of my own feelings."

She said nothing more and he thought she had fallen asleep. He stretched out, the bow and arrow behind his head, his sword beside his right hand. He let his limbs relax, though he did not intend to sleep.

After a little while Aki's voice surprised him. "I am dedicated to be a shrine maiden. I promised my father that I would not let any man be intimate with me, that I would kill him. I still have my knife. I am just warning you."

"Go to sleep," he said, but he wished she had not brought up the subject. Now he was even more aware of the female body next to his. Memories of the day's events seemed to race through his muscles and his veins. First he had killed two men, dropping them like hares. Then Kon had attacked Zen and torn the other werehawk to pieces, and Shika had understood his speech and had wrested him from the Prince Abbot's control. He had walked between the worlds at the crossroads, had spoken to the spirit of the Kuromori lord, and had summoned it from the entrance of Hell into the foal's developing body.

Truly I am a sorcerer of power! Of what else am I capable?

Pride began to well up in him, sweet and seductive, telling him he deserved all things, that he was allowed all things, that he could take what he wanted, in this world and the next. This was the one meant for him, the one the sorceress had told him he would wed. She was here, alongside him. He had killed for her, he had rescued her.

The night was warm, filled with the sounds of spring, frogs croaking from the stream, insects calling. The lute continued to play quietly, its plangent notes adding to his desire.

He turned restlessly and then sat up, deciding to meditate for a while to try to still his rebellious body. He fumbled in the dark for the seven-layered bag, took out the mask, and slipped it over his face.

Immediately he felt himself transported from the hut, bounding on stag's hoofs toward Ryusonji. He struggled to take control, reached inside himself for Sesshin's power. He stood on the veranda of the temple and saw the Prince Abbot, sitting in meditation by the open door.

The priest said without opening his eyes, "So, my little stag has returned? Did you think you would escape me so easily?"

Shika tried to regain his will, to turn and run, but his limbs were frozen as if he were dreaming.

"Where is Prince Yoshimori? If you have found him why have you not brought me his head? What have you been doing and how did you evade me before, at the crossroads?"

The Prince Abbot opened his eyes and stood, and Shika felt the full force of his rage.

"I will punish you," the priest said. "You dare to try to

oppose me? You have no idea how strong I am. Now go and do what you want with the Autumn Princess. I see your lust for her. Take her now, why wait for marriage? Then kill Yoshimori and bring me his head."

The Prince Abbot raised his hand and spoke words Shika had never heard before. He found himself back in the hut. The power of the forest was all around him and the pure animal instinct of the stag swept over him. The girl turned in her sleep toward him. Her robe was open. Then she was in his arms and his mouth was on hers. She tried to push him away, he remembered briefly the knife, but then nothing would stop him, neither pity nor fear. He possessed her as the stag does the hind, with mindless domination. But even as he cried out at the moment of ecstasy, he realized what the Prince Abbot had done, and he had the first inkling of how complete his punishment would be.

He wrenched off the mask and threw it from him. She lay without moving or speaking. He wanted to hold her and caress her with tenderness, but shame prevented him. He pulled his clothes around him and went to the door of the hut. Beyond him lay the Darkwood and all the sounds and shadows of the nighttime forest. Far away, wolves were howling. He recalled his earlier pride and exultation with despair and disgust. He went a little way down the side of the hut and leaned against the rough-sawn planks of the wall. He had no idea what to do now. He just knew he had failed.

From the hut he thought he heard sounds of weeping,

but the lute was still playing softly, so he could not be sure. His own eyes grew hot, but he would not grant himself the relief of tears. He walked away into the darkness, stumbling over fallen branches, until he came up against the trunk of a huge cedar. He clasped it in his arms and leaned his forehead against it, then slid to its base, feeling the moss cool against his skin.

When he came to his senses it was dawn. He made himself get up and return to the hut. He was not sure what he would do: throw himself down before her, ask for forgiveness, seek her help. But she was not there. Had his actions forced her to run away, to abandon Yoshimori? He turned and called her name, "Akihime! Akihime!"

Birds were singing and Kon answered them from the rooftop. Rain was falling softly, a drizzling mist that hid the mountains. He knew he had lost her, a loss that felt immeasurable, as if it encompassed the whole world. Every tree dripped with moisture as though they wept with him. He had not rescued her. How arrogant to think that! She had been entrusted to him and he had broken that trust. He called again, "Akihime!"

The horses whinnied in response to his voice, and at the same moment he heard something stir in the hut. Was she there, had he somehow overlooked her? He went inside.

The boy was awake, staring at him with puzzled eyes.

"Where is Aki . . . older sister?" he said.

"I don't know. She's gone. She ran away."

Yoshi's gaze remained steady. "Where to? Why did she leave me? What have you done to her?"

The mask lay on the floor, staring at him with its hollow eyes. Hardly knowing what he was doing, but seeking some relief from his remorse and regret, he picked it up and put it on. Immediately he felt the pull of the Prince Abbot's power, and knew what he must do. Perhaps it would assuage his immense pain. Yoshimori would never have become emperor anyway. His family were all dead and those who would have fought for him scattered. Now Shikanoko had to put an end to his life and take his handsome head back to Ryusonji.

He picked up his sword and held his hand out to the boy.

Yoshimori shrank from the sight of the mask.

"Come, Your Majesty must be brave," Shika said.

"Shall I bring the lute?" Yoshi asked.

"There is no need for it," Shika replied, and led him out of the hut.

The rain continued to fall softly, the birds were silent, and there was no wind. The only sound was the rushing water and the pounding of Shika's heart. It was not the riverbank at Miyako, where so many were taken to be executed, but the side of a mountain stream, which would serve equally well.

"Look away from me toward the mountains," he commanded.

After one brief glance Yoshi obeyed him.

As Shika raised his sword, Yoshi said, "The sun is rising."

How could he see it? Clouds covered the sky, but the sun's rays must have penetrated them in some way, for the raindrops were reflecting the colors of the rainbow all around them. For a moment Shika was dazzled, seeing clearly the fragile beauty of the child before him. He hesitated, suddenly reluctant to do what he was supposed to do.

From the cave came the twang of a bow. Time stopped. The world held its breath, the sword outlined against the fractured light. Shika gripped it harder and inhaled deeply.

Kon swooped toward him, talons extended, beak slashing, and the horses burst from the cave, Risu leading, her teeth bared, her ears flat.

Shika dropped the sword, raising his arms to protect the mask. Kon seized it in his talons, tore it from Shika's face, and let it fall as Risu charged him, knocking him to the ground. He had seen her bad tempered before and she had bitten and kicked him many times, but he had never seen her so enraged she wanted to kill him. Nyorin was also lunging at him as he struggled to his feet, the stallion's lips drawn back from his huge white teeth, his eyes flashing as if in the midst of battle. Nyorin's head, solid bone, collided with Shika's and as he fell again the stallion whirled around, kicking him with both back legs.

Neither sorcery nor all his skill with weapons could help him. Risu seized his right arm in her teeth and snapped it. Nyorin kicked him again, then brought his forefeet down on him, striking him on neck and shoulder. The mask lay on the ground, shattered in two. His vision went red with pain and then black.

When he regained consciousness the rain was falling

more heavily. He crawled to the water and lay in it, feeling its icy coldness on every cut and bruise. One eye was closing and he could hardly see out of the other, yet he knew Yoshimori and the horses were gone. He could not raise his head to look upward to see if Kon had gone, too, but there was no sound from the werehawk. His arm throbbed unbearably and he could not move it, but the bone had not broken through the skin.

He began to tremble, not only from the cold water and the pain but also from profound shock that the horses he had loved and trusted should turn on him. He could understand why Kon had attacked him as viciously as he had gone for Zen—the werehawk's instinct to protect the Emperor overrode any commands from either Shika or the Prince Abbot. But the horses? After many more minutes of confusion and pain the realization came to him that it was Kiyoyori's spirit, within the unborn foal, that had driven Risu to turn on him, and Nyorin had followed.

Even the animal world recognizes that Yoshimori is emperor, and fights for him, he thought.

Eventually he managed to stand. He picked up the sword with his left hand and went to the hut. He could hardly bear to enter it—it seemed to reverberate still with his uncontrolled lust and he heard again his own cries with revulsion.

He gathered up the bow and the quiver of arrows, and the twisted metal that had been Kiyoyori's sword. The lute had gone—of course it would have gone with Yoshi: not only animals but also objects recognized him.

Outside, he picked up the pieces of the broken mask and put them in the brocade seven-layered bag. He would go into the Darkwood. It would either kill him or heal him. If it healed him he would see the Prince Abbot destroyed and Yoshimori on the Lotus Throne.

AUTHOR'S NOTE

The Tale of Shikanoko was partly inspired by the great medieval warrior tales of Japan: *The Tale of the Heike*, *The Taiheiki*, the tales of Hōgen and Heiji, the *Jōkyūki*, and *The Tale of the Soga Brothers*. I have borrowed descriptions of weapons and clothes from these and am indebted to their English translators Royall Tyler, Helen Craig McCullough, and Thomas J. Cogan.

I would like to thank in particular Randy Schadel, who read early versions of the novels and made many invaluable suggestions.

All four volumes of Lian Hearn's
The Tale of Shikanoko will be published in 2016.

EMPEROR OF THE EIGHT ISLANDS
April 2016

AUTUMN PRINCESS, DRAGON CHILD
June 2016

LORD OF THE DARKWOOD
August 2016

THE TENGU'S GAME OF GO
September 2016

FSG Originals
www.fsgoriginals.com